he's all that

he's all that

RENÉE ALEXIS

KENSINGTON BOOKS
http://www.kensingtonbooks.com

KENSINGTON BOOKS are published by

Kensington Publishing Corp.
850 Third Avenue
New York, NY 10022

ISBN: 0-7582-1482-0

First Kensington Trade Paperback Printing: June 2006

10   9   8   7   6   5   4   3   2   1

Printed in the United States of America

in too deep

Finally, Wayne State University was offering Thursday evening swim classes in the new athletic building. Eve Harlan was a nine-to-fiver, and her hectic schedule wouldn't permit her to do anything but work and go back home pretty much all week, every week. There were always meetings, staff functions, and last-minute problems with customers. Being a manager at Blue Cross and Blue Shield, there was never any time to take care of things that weren't last minute, except on Thursdays.

Thursdays were hers, and she booked with lightning speed from her downtown office to get on with life—hopefully, soon to come, an exciting life. She could only wish upon one of the many stars dotting the January sky in Detroit that her *exciting life* would hurry the hell up and make an appearance.

Wishing upon a star was exactly what Eve did last October, and that wish had produced a trip to the Bahamas for the coming April. Yes, finally, she and her best girlfriend Margo were to leave Detroit's cold, early spring behind and strut their stuff in front of the first man who crossed their path on one of the many beaches they planned on discovering. But before that could happen, changes had to be made. Not changes in their schedule; that was a done deal; not any changes in clothing that were already packed and waiting in a suitcase.

The change was something big time, enormous, life changing. Including dropping a few pounds so she, and Margo for that matter, wouldn't look like beached whales that children hovered around and poked sticks into. Eve wanted to be really ready and hoped that another kind of stick would be poked into her—hot, thick, and slammin' boners, from hot and slammin' hunks. There was only one way to assure that—no more pizzas loaded with everything imaginable, including two kinds of cheese. That was the killer. What would she do without her double doses of Swiss and Parmesan?

When Margo, who still insisted that she looked great in a thong bikini while wearing a size twenty—women's— decided she had to have pizza or die and offered to pay, Eve's response was a stiff no. Though Eve was nowhere near a size twenty, she wanted to look really svelte in her orange and lime green two-piece that showed off an ass to kill for. The only problem was getting that ass!

The solution, other than staying away from pizza, was Wayne State University on Thursday evenings. She'd wanted to see the new facility, having passed it millions of times on the Lodge Freeway getting to work. She'd heard talk of how wonderful it was, with all the new state-of-the-art exercise equipment. She needed that but never knew she didn't have to be a student there to use the facilities. What better way to get her ass in shape than to learn to swim in a new Olympic-size pool?

There was only one more little problem: trudging through the snow and cold to get there. It was terribly cold outside that particular night, like January in Detroit usually was, and her first mind told her to give it up that night. *Go home and max out to Lifetime television with a bowl of popcorn*—with *butter.* Her sane mind said, *you paid the ten dollars for the swim class, so get that almost flabby ass over there. Now!*

With a hasty foot on the accelerator of her recently purchased Mercedes L-class, she arrived. Eve walked into the new building and looked around. It was as gorgeous as everyone said: blue-green glass windows all over the place, exotic plants here and there, new techno-furniture in the lounging areas, and, of course, a giant health bar situated by the miniature cascading water fountain. Eve was impressed, amazed and all of a sudden couldn't wait to get into the pool, after years of avoiding them.

She walked down the long blue-green carpeted hallway and could hear the water before she got to the locker rooms. It sounded nice, kind of tropical and soothing. Everything she needed in her hectic life.

Eve entered the changing area, found an empty locker in the elaborately large room, and suited up. She looked over at the other students also suiting up and knew she purely had nothing to worry about. Some just sprawled across the benches wearing clothing way too tight in every thinkable place. She hoped they were going to the aerobics class down the hall from the pool.

Eve slid into her two-piece, which looked outstanding against her bronze skin and long, reddish hair. She took one last look at herself in the mirror to make sure everything was inside the bathing suit and took off for the pool. There was no way in hell she was going to embarrass herself by walking into a room full of people with flab hanging out anywhere. She'd rather stay home, enjoy the buttered popcorn, and get fat in peace.

Moments after stepping into the knee-deep water, which, by the way, she considered too deep for her liking, three of the women from the locker room walked in and jumped into the pool. She closed her eyes for a second, thinking that the water was sure to splash out and cover all four walls, especially once she stepped in. True, the thought was rude, but it was funny to her, and that's all that mattered. When you live in a city where you turned into an Eskimo for four out of twelve months, you have to find some kind of comfort food, and a dose of levity didn't hurt either. Her life surely hadn't been anything to laugh about lately.

The man she was originally supposed to go on the trip with, along with Margo, found loving comfort in the arms of another woman—in Eve's own apartment, at that. Needless to say, his part of the trip was cancelled, and she immediately spent some of his money on the new swimsuit, swim classes, and a tune-up for the Mercedes. That oughta teach a dude to cheat on a fly-girl like her.

She stood in her corner of the pool, fixing her straps, and secretly high-fived herself for not looking like a human flotation device, despite the amount of food she personally consumed. Eve smiled, imagining how quickly she and those women could have sunk the *Titanic* just by stepping aboard. Dismissing the thought before it got her in trouble, she relaxed and stayed in her little corner, awaiting the instructor.

Then he appeared. At least Eve was hoping that fine hunk of human DNA was him. He stood on the side of the pool and sized everyone up. There were only four women in the pool, and they all looked googly-eyed at him. The guy was hooked up from the floor up and just about the prettiest guy in creation. Normally white men weren't her thing, but this one made every man she'd ever seen look like Laurel and Hardy. She couldn't wait for him to crawl into that pool and see just how scrumptious he looked wet.

He got in, treaded to the middle of the pool like he had been born in one, and started his evening. Walking through that water was a breeze to him. He had long, masculine thighs that quarters could bounce from. They looked so hot, as if he could trap a woman between those thighs and squeeze all kinds of pleasure into her. The thought of it made Eve wetter than the pool had. He introduced himself as Jordan Whittaker, dipped his head into the water to acclimate himself to the temperature, and came up looking like an outrageously seductive stud muffin. His trunks tented in the front like someone had just gone down on him. At that point, he was okay with Eve. A male instructor and HOT enough to heat the water. Her evening was starting out fucking great. Those tiny trunks left nothing to the imagination, and Eve's was on over-drive. His inches were already in the action mode. To Eve, the action mode was when the erection pokes out so far that it touches the stars and moon. And this man was packin' in a major way.

When he got into the water, all that wavy strawberry-blond hair turned dark, and those hard muscles contracted from the cold water. His chest was so chiseled that the four women could do nothing but follow his scent, like tracking dogs. Of course, following a tight butt like that was simply their pleasure. They all smiled at one another behind his back and kept pace with him. As fine as he was, they would have followed him into a tidal wave, and he was fine enough to prevent rational thinking. They did, however, manage to hear him say it was a beginner class and that they'd start out with simple leg exercises and floating techniques. Eve was all too ready to do any exercise with Mr. Whittaker and would have been glad to bend into a human pretzel for him.

Once into his first lesson, Eve couldn't understand how he managed to lift each of the others to get them to float on their backs. But he was strong. She watched the muscles in his arms flex as he lifted them, and it was to die for.

He got everyone adjusted to the water and made them feel that it was their friend. Hell. Her turn next. The last thing Eve wanted was to make friends with fifteen feet of water. She wanted to be nice and friendly with him and on every part of his delicious, slick body. No harm in fantasizing about it . . .

Jordan was a little uneasy about approaching her. From the moment he'd entered the pool, his eyes had been on her, and he wondered how in hell he'd manage to teach her anything other than the art of screwing in a major way. Noticing how succulent she looked certainly wasn't helping him. The way her breasts looked in that push-up suit with nice, pokey nipples dotting it made his inches hotter and stiffer than actually getting screwed. And she was just as scrumptious from behind, sporting a suit with high cut legs, showing off the most tantalizing derriere he'd seen in, well, ages! However, his job was to teach her to swim and not eat her out royally, so he tried to dismiss the thought of being between her thighs and began to instruct her on leg exercises. His erection remained, however.

Eve was just as attracted to him, and her eyes couldn't be peeled from the intense tenting in his trunks. For a white dude, his inches were smoking. Jordan Whittaker was his own porn movie, and she, a willing costar.

Since he looked delicious enough to marinate in, she was willing to do anything he told her—until their next set of instructions was announced. Floating on her back had always scared the hell out of her. In fact, water alone scared her; gave her bad memories of what had happened in her cousin's backyard when she was seven years old. Sure, that had been twenty years ago, but the memory was still alive in her mind. But Jordan Whittaker wouldn't be a bad memory; in fact, he would be a good one, especially his tight trunks that were putting a killin' on her hot, throbbing sex. OK. She'd give floating a chance and see where it took her.

Jordan saw the reluctance on her face as he approached her. "You don't have a lot of experience with water, do you?"

"A little." Telling Jordan that she and water didn't mix, for reasons she didn't want to get into, was a no-no. He'd treat her with caution and barely give her anything to do. The last thing she wanted was sympathy. She wanted to learn how to swim no matter what. Eve wanted all the men in the Bahamas, but that could wait. Right now the one she wanted was Mr. Jordan H. Whittaker, with the H standing for hot as hell!

Jordan held his hands out to Eve, enticing her deeper into the water. "Take my hands and tread out a little farther with me. You can't float very well in water that's too shallow, darling."

Darling. Was she his darling? She sure wanted to be, but

nerves tingled throughout her body. "I'm . . . I'm just a bit scared."

"Nothing to be scared of, sweetheart. I've got you, and I won't let anything happen."

"You sure you'll hold on to me?"

"I'll hold you so tight you'll beg me to let go. Come on, once you get the hang of it, you won't need Jordan Whittaker anymore."

The hell I won't. "Well, if you're sure about this."

"I'm very sure. See over there? They're doing it." He moved in closer to her, practically whispering, "Your body is way lighter and sexier than theirs. If they can do it, I know you'll float like a stick." *A joy stick.* "Come in deeper, the water's great."

The minute his hands slid to her backside and she lifted up, Jordan knew the class would be a thrill. His tenting trunks were indicative of that. He moved in closer, feeling her wet, warm flesh tracing his. He tried concentrating on getting her to float, but what he really wanted to do was float on top of her, behind her, inside of her. The idea of lifting her legs to the sky and pounding like a jackhammer between those parted thighs was putting him in a trance. He knew he had to get it together because letting a student know he was attracted to her was grounds for getting fired. After all, he didn't know if she liked him the same way or not. He saw her eyes roam across his tight abs and lower body, but all women did that to him no matter if he had on the Speedos or the trunks.

He cleared his voice and directed her. "Now, relax in my arms with the idea that you are floating on a cloud. Arch your back and slowly begin to wave your arms." He watched as she followed his instructions to the letter. Her arching back resting against his hands made his mind race with thoughts of sucking those perky nipples, now closer than ever to him. "Good girl. You're doing great. Relax a little more."

To stop himself from staring into her gorgeous light brown eyes, he looked over at his other students practicing their kick-offs from the ledge of the pool and called to them. "Give me a minute longer with this student. I want to see legs kicking harder, ladies."

As he spoke to the others, Eve caught a good look at him. He was just plain beautiful; keen facial features with full, juicy lips and dark green eyes to fucking kill for. The thing about it was, Eve felt safe with him as well as being on the verge of having a momentous orgasm. He was strong, sexy, pretty, and such a good teacher. He took away most of her fears about the water. Most of them.

She still wanted him to stay near her if a sudden case of the spooks took over. More importantly, his hands felt incredible on her, barely moving up and down the open part of the swimsuit, rubbing her tender flesh with the pads of his fingers. She didn't know if his hand movements were conscious or subconscious. All she knew was that it felt out of this fucking world. Eve couldn't help but imagine what his incredibly thick rod could do to her. From the looks of it, it could take her on a magic carpet ride and fly her straight into "getting done-in royally USA!"

When Eve's eyes and mind returned to reality, Jordan was staring at her. She was so embarrassed because she knew there was a pleased little smile on her face.

Jordan pretended not to notice and smiled back at her. "Are you feeling comfortable?"

"Extremely."

"Good girl. Now I'm going to let go."

"What?"

"Don't panic. I'll still be here, right by your side, only my fingers will be resting in the water, directly under you. Are you okay with that?"

"I won't know until I try it first."

"See, you're even more confident than before. Okay, try it, and remember, I'm right here, sweetheart."

There was that word again, and she loved how it rolled from his tongue. He didn't call anyone that but her. She was privileged and King Jordan gave it to her. *If only he could give me more, let me take more and drain his pool until he was bone dry.* The idea of his moist lips on hers, sucking her, licking her, and landing his wet, taut body on top of hers, swaying his hips up and down on her in erotic form did wonders for her morale. Dreams, only dreams. This swim class was only going to last three weeks. He'd never know how much she desired him.

What was she doing? Her mind was gone, totally taking her attention from her lessons and increasing her chance of drowning. *No. He'd never let that happen to me.* At that, she stiffened her back, gave him one more look of confidence, then tried floating alone.

Jordan watched as she stayed afloat on her own, smiling at her ability to really do it. "See, I told you that you could do it. Already a pro, and with a body like yours, you'll float like driftwood." Then he thought about his words. "What I meant about your body was—"

"It's okay, Mr. Whittaker. I know what you're saying. And if anyone's the pro here, it's you."

"Not a pro, just a man who loves two things, water and beautiful women."

"Then being here with me must be a drag."

"Not exactly what was on my mind. Listen, Eve, if I don't help the other students soon, you'll see just what I mean." He slid his hand back under her, supporting her back. He could see her muscles tensing, becoming tired. "For the time being, just relax against me. Float and think about resting on a cloud."

"A cloud of hot, wet muscles? Easy to do."

She had barely gotten the hang of floating and told him she wasn't secure yet. He stayed with her a little longer, pretending to concentrate on her arching back, while in reality, her breasts bouncing to the flow of the water was killing him. Not to mention the hard nipples that swelled against her suit. A slight smile covered his wonderfully sensual lips. His feverish erection barely pressed against her lower back, and was getting even harder. "A few minutes on your stomach will help you get more adjusted to the water. Wanna try it?"

"You'll be with me?"

"Every inch of the way." And he meant that literally.

So as not to further embarrass himself, Jordan turned her onto her stomach, still supporting her but getting a good look at a nice, juicy ass and feminine, but muscular thighs. He felt himself about to get in too deep, wanting to slide her suit off and nail her in five feet of water, visible to any and all things on the planet. Instead, he placed her feet on the bottom of the pool. "I really need to go and help the other ladies. They're getting tired of leg kicks."

Jordan quickly treaded through the water, returning to the other side of the pool where the others were, asking for help they seemingly didn't need. But Eve needed all he could teach her and all he could fill her with.

His arousal was not unnoticed; she had brushed against the flaming erection that felt like it wanted to blister her insides, up and down and all night long. Yes, Eve knew the attraction was on. She could see him glance her way, wanting to smile at her but fearing to in front of the other women. She knew the deal and was perfectly okay with kicking from the side of the pool to strengthen her thighs. He'd return to her soon, and she knew that. That fabulously engorged erection of his would gladly lead the way.

From the other side of the pool, Jordan was scoping her, practically wagging his tongue at how hard she was kicking, spreading her legs and arching her back. What he'd do to be between those perfect creamy brown thighs would be illegal. Yes, he'd rob to get to her, then rob her—of any and all come that she could produce. He loved women dearly, and setting eyes on her totally proved that, but he also loved his job; a job that a rock like hard-on was getting in the way of. Still, he was dead set on keeping everything professional.

Eve continued to watch him as he demonstrated the use of

the flotation devices. Watching him as he put the flotation pad in the water and climbed aboard looked so enticing. He made it look so easy, just hopping aboard, no falling over, no sliding off, just natural with it. He was a human fish—and she wanted fish for dinner. Watching Jordan maneuver that device around made her wish she were a flotation board. The thought of him on top of her was making her core explode in the most erotic ways. She was aching for the guy, and stripping out of everything right in the pool was a serious temptation.

That was when Eve decided she had to get out of there because she wasn't concentrating on the lessons; too many distractions. She would pick another night to learn how to swim. She wouldn't learn a thing from Jordan except how to screw in water. From the way it looked, Jordan wasn't planning on screwing his student, so she dragged herself to the steps and walked up.

Jordan called to her from the middle of the pool. "Ms. Harlan, where are you going? The lesson isn't over."

Everyone in the pool was looking at her. "It is for me. I just don't think I'm cut out for this."

He walked to the edge and looked up at her. "I beg to differ. You were doing so well with your floating."

"Sure, as long as you were there to help me. The minute you let go, all of my fears returned." That wasn't it, and she knew it. What she was doing was dodging him. Without even trying, he was taking her body on a journey to mystical places, and he was hard to fight. The idea of fucking him until she was in a literal frenzy was taking over.

Jordan approached even closer, so close that he wasn't audible to the others, trying to lure her back into his liquid lair. "How do you know it isn't for you? The class isn't over yet and it could be fun." He stepped back a bit, and she swore that the erection inside his navy trunks was calling her, enticing her back inside. He took her hand. "You can do this. I know what you're going through, and I hope I'm the reason."

That took her mind away from everything. "What do you mean?"

"Every time I look at you, my trunks fit a little tighter, but we can get through this and remain professional, right?"

"You read faces really well, don't you?"

"So do you. C'mon, give it another try. After that, if you can't deal, you don't have to come back. I'll miss you, though. You're a good student."

"I am? I just got here."

"Doesn't matter. I'm satisfied with your learning ability."

It was the way he said *satisfied* that got her back into the pool. The fact that he took her hand and led her back in didn't hurt either. His hands were so warm, despite the coolness of the water. That made Eve wonder just how warm everything else was on him. The idea of it turned the seat of her suit into watery Jello, but she tried to hide it.

Ten minutes later, Jordan dismissed class, and Eve walked away knowing that she, at least, did learn how to float. She started up the steps behind the other women when he called out. She turned and saw him still standing in knee-deep water, sporting that juicy erection. He looked like testosterone heaven, and Eve loved the sight of him. Her barely controlled voice responded back to him. "Yes, Mr. Whittaker?"

"You can call me Jordan now. The others are gone. Those few minutes you were out of the pool you missed something."

"Yeah, like what?" She really didn't care. All she wanted was to get back in the pool with him anyway.

"You missed the workout on the flotation device."

The way he said that made her think of how Prince sang "International Lover," eroticism done right! Needless to say, Eve jumped back in and treaded over to him. He met her and took her hand. "You'll need to have this experience, Ms. Harlan."

"It might be helpful for my trip this summer. By the way, you can call me Eve. And how did you know who I was? There were four women in the pool."

"I study names and match them with faces. You had to be Eve because you look like you belong in the Garden of Eden."

"Awfully fancy words for a swim instructor, Jordan."

"Well, I teach literature and English on this campus during the day. C'mon on, let's go deeper and test out those devices."

"No, I'm scared of deep water."

"We won't go too deep." His eyes searched her up and down. "Well, I might go deep."

Her legs went weak. Thank God the door automatically locked after the others left because *it* was about to happen. No going back now.

Eve followed him into water that was above her chest but only to his upper stomach because he was so tall. She didn't like being in that deep. "I don't think I like this, Jordan." Her voice echoed off the tile walls.

"I'm right here with you, and we won't go any farther. Do you trust me?"

"Of course I trust you."

"Can I do a few things to you?"

That made her smile beyond rhyme or reason. "Do things to me?"

"What I mean is, can I show you a few things?"

"You can show me whatever you like."

"That's too enticing, Eve, but I meant this." He placed her hands on the edge of the pool and moved in behind her with the flotation pad. His husky voice murmured, "Now, watch this." He let go of the side, slid on top of the board and rested there. "All you have to do is relax on it. Think you might want to try?"

"Will you hang on to me?"

"My pleasure."

He put her arms around his shoulders and moved her into the middle of the pool where her feet couldn't touch the bottom. It felt out of this world hanging on to him; he was warm and tight, just how she liked a man. The fact that his inches were flush against her stomach made her want to keep hanging on to him.

He pulled the board over to her and lifted her on top of it. Eve fell off almost immediately and went completely under.

Jordan dipped under and brought her up. She was coughing and gasping for air. He took her to the side and wiped the strands of hair from her face. "Are you okay? I'm sorry that happened." His eyes narrowed in on her heaving chest as he spoke, wanting and feeling excited by the sight but more concerned for her safety. "Maybe we should quit for the night." He walked her to the shallow part of the pool.

"No! No, I like it in here with you. I feel comfortable, actually, and I really need to learn these things to overcome my fear."

"What fear is that?"

"I don't want to get into it right now. It's a long, sad story."

He moved in closer to her, so close that she could see the tiny laugh lines on the corners of his perfect mouth. "Maybe one day you'll tell me."

"I'd like to, but first I should learn about that flotation thing."

"You aren't scared to go back in?"

Her arms circled around his shoulders again. "I'm fine, really."

He moistened his lower lip with his tongue. "I know you're fine. The minute I looked at you in that water, a massive hard-on attacked me. It's still there."

Bold words. But she was bolder. Now standing in barely two feet of water, Eve cupped his scrotum. The massage her hand gave him made him buck against her. His shaft was so hard and thick that she immediately came from the thought of him inside her. Once returning to reality, she smiled at him. "I'm going out on a limb saying this to a stranger, but I've never wanted a man as much and as deep as I want you.

I want you to fill me, Jordan, make me pop. Explode all over me."

"Is that what you want? Because I'm so willing to give it, Eve. I want you to really want it, though. Give in and let me do whatever I want to and for however long it takes. But first . . ." He hauled himself out of the pool and grabbed two dry towels, soaking them in the water and then whapping them in high throws over the security cameras. "There. Now we have privacy. Let's do it."

He jumped back into the pool and teased her, giving her a succulent, juicy kiss, parting her lips and dancing his tongue around hers. It felt so good that they just kept going.

He slid the suit straps off her shoulders, exposing more of her bare skin. He caressed her neck and shoulders as he continued to slide the suit farther down. The minute her breasts were exposed, his lips attacked them, sucking nipples that swelled even more under his tongue bath. The more he sucked and massaged them with the water bouncing across them, the harder they became.

He moved down her stomach and poked his tongue in and out of her navel. "That tastes so damn good, Eve. Everything on you tastes good, the way I knew it would."

"It gets better."

"Yeah, well, let me taste it." That was only the icing on the cake because when he lowered her bottoms and thrust two very long fingers into her throbbing core, she almost left the planet. He moved his fingers into her so deeply that she could feel him touching her soul. Her hips matched his tempo, and she swore his length was about to spill out of those trunks. Eve helped it along.

While rocking his fingers vigorously inside of her, she reached for his trunks, but they were so slippery that she couldn't peel them off without help. He stood up and slid them off. Good God! The sight of that pretty, pumping nightstick unleashed made her immediately drop to her knees. She wrapped her hand around a shaft so beautiful and thick that she could barely believe her eyes.

His back arched with pleasure, and he started moaning, "Do it, sugar. Take it; put it between those sexy lips of yours."

Hell, who wouldn't obey a command like that? She massaged his smooth, silky shaft with her thumb. The veins got harder and longer on it and she knew she had to have Jordan tickling the back of her throat. If he tasted as good as he looked, she knew she was in for the dessert of a lifetime; way better than the popcorn and the Lifetime movie she would have been snuggling up to.

He urged her again. "Suck it, baby. Aah, just like that. It feels so damn good."

Oh yes! She slowly inched him in until the back of her throat was full of him. Then she moved him in and out, slowly, squeezing him, tickling his scrotum with her nails and waxing his shaft like she was out of control. She was. No man had ever tasted that good to her. Eve didn't know why, but she figured he was just awful damn good by nature. He swelled so large that she couldn't fit him all in. She knew for sure then that her sex was in for a good workout.

As if reading her mind, he slowly pulled her up and kissed her lips again, whispering, "That felt so fucking good, sweetheart. Now it's time for yours." He stepped out of his trunks and hoisted her to the tile. Before Eve knew anything, her thighs were spread far apart, and his tongue was dipping inside of her, swirling around in there like he was lapping up her entire core. It felt so outstanding that her entire body was tensing. He held on and wrapped his strong arms around her legs to keep her in place. He ate his darling Eve out like wild and sent her on a journey way beyond reality in waves of passion.

The man couldn't have taught English; it damn well had to be biology because he was freakin' on her with such expertise, exploring everything even the naked eye couldn't see.

Eve's juices slowly dripped all over him, but he kept sucking, twirling his tongue in circles all over her core, draining the life out of her. Arching her back for him was surely her pleasure. Suddenly the pool and the others sharing the class with her were but a faint memory. All that existed was Jordan Whittaker, the only man she'd be pleased to drown for, as long as she was drowning in him.

After moments of orally screwing the daylights out of her, he mounted her and slid that wonderful shaft into her in one swift slide, feeling her adjust immediately to his size. He rocked slowly at first, almost pulling out, then teased her until he plunged back in completely again. It was like he was making up for lost time with her, like no one lately had given him what he needed, what he craved, and he took it all out on Eve. He rocked in and out, hard, heavily, for a good twenty minutes. He had stamina like crazy.

She came so many times that she thought she was going to die from rapture. Eve had heard of women passing out from ecstasy and couldn't understand that at first, but now being party to it, it made perfect sense. No one had given it up to her like that before; certainly not the dude she caught screwing someone in her own apartment. It would take the most delicious white man in the galaxy to take her beyond the stars. From that point on, her favorite color was cream—for the cream she knew he'd soon spill if he continued shaking, rattling, and rolling with her.

Jordan's muscles tensed again. He bucked against her, called and shouted her name at the top of his lungs, and took them both skyrocketing in a fusion of heat, desire, and total passion. Jordan pulled out and then spewed creamy nectar all over her breasts and stomach, massaging it into her skin with long, smooth finger strokes. Eve's eyes rolled in ecstasy as he caressed her skin with his satiny liquid. "Was that good, baby?"

"Amazing. No man has ever felt that good to me before."

He kissed her again, long and deep, then rolled off. Damn,

his erection was still so hard. Eve guessed that it took a well-tuned body like his much longer to come down from a high like that.

He helped her to her feet and wrapped her in his arms again. They both looked into the water just in time to see both his trunks and her suit floating away. She smiled. "How are we going to get those back?"

"I'll either swim out or get that pole over there to retrieve them later."

He took her hand and led her toward the closest shower stalls, the men's showers.

Eve looked at the sign above the entrance. "Won't we get caught in here? I will look a little awkward in a men's shower."

"No one is here but us. My class is the last class of the evening."

"This scenario sounds a little too good to be true. Are you sure you didn't plan this?"

"Positive, but I have planned something else. Care to engage me?"

They showered together that night. That poor shower stall filled with heat as he filled Eve with his. What made it even more earth-shattering was how he used the soap to send her body into an unknown zone. Their bodies were nice and hot from lovemaking. He took the bar of soap, circled her breasts, midsection, and behind, and massaged it in and went from there. His delicate strokes cleansed every part of her in an exquisitely sensual way.

Once he soaped her down, he leaned her into the water, caressing the soap away. The pleasure was so intense, building inside of her, making her ache for release. He knew this but told her to hang on a little longer, to let the water and the caresses stimulate her in preparation for the ultimate moment.

His slippery fingers found her aching mound, massaged her, making her clit hot and throbbing, but not so much that she caved in; he knew when to stop, knew when her body had had enough temptation. He nibbled her neck and shoulders as his member moved up and down across her stomach.

Eve pulled away slowly, staring into those perfect green eyes. "Jordan, now, now."

"No. I want it pent up so tightly within you that you kill me with your release. I want you to give it all to me, make me suffer, much like I did when I first saw you and couldn't immediately have you."

"Please, Jordan, I can barely stand it. I need to feel your deepness again."

He removed his portable shower bag from the hook and took out a hairbrush. Eve looked at it, wondering what the hell he was going to do with it. "Jordan, what's—?"

He quietly said into her ear, "Hush, darling, you'll love this."

She felt the rubber handle move across her stomach and onto her slick mound. The wet rubber felt so damn good between her thighs, and her punanny was so slippery from her own moisture that the handle slid easily into her. He rocked it in and out, forcing Eve's back against the wall as the small brush stimulated her. He smiled at her pleasure. "Do you like how it feels?"

"Don't talk, Jordan. Just keep doing it."

At that, he retracted it, sliding it slowly in and out, moving it from side to side to make sure her clit felt everything it needed to feel. She came in waves that spiraled within her, wetting the handle of the brush with juices from a core that was simply getting nailed. He soon retracted the brush and slid its tiny feathery bristles against the baby-soft hair covering her center. The more he stroked her, the harder she kissed him, trying to talk between kisses. "Slide something back into me, Jordan. You know what I mean."

He hoisted her up, and her legs encircled his hips. With a few thrusts and moans, Jordan was back inside, making the brush's bristles and his delicious cock burst her wide open as it did double duty. Her orgasm came down on her so hard that she scratched up and down his back, and her hands were red from pounding them against the tile.

Jordan came all over the place again, wetting her with his sweet stream, practically from head to toe. Once he recovered, he lowered her to the ground and kissed her once again. He broke away from her and stared at the clock on the opposite side of the wall. "We'd better go before they close the place. You'd be trapped in here with me, and I'd be merciless toward you, Ms. Harlan."

"I'd expect nothing less."

"Will you come back next Thursday? I can show you some new techniques in the water; some I'm sure you'll want to use when you go on your trip."

"No. I'll save those moves for you, only you."

"I'm glad." He looked at the clock again. "Let me take you back to the dressing room. We can meet in the hallway, and I'll walk you to your car. Sound like a plan?"

"An excellent one, Jordan, and I think I can find my way to the ladies' dressing room. If I need help, I'll call you. I may call you, anyway."

"You have been for over an hour, anyway. What's to stop you now?"

Eve backed away, staring at him, then disappeared behind the door.

Jordan looked down at his still engorged erection, feeling the stiff tip as he stroked it. "Eve, you're a hell of a student."

The warm shower helped that determined cock relax, but each time he thought of the beautiful woman behind the other wall, something stirred in him, and the erection started its ascent. One way or another, it had to stay down or his suit pants wouldn't fit, and going out into January weather with an open fly didn't sound appetizing.

Almost an hour later, Eve stepped from the women's locker room sporting her winter white business suit with the sparkling red blouse underneath, a pair of matching beige heels, and her hair blow-dried to perfection. With her makeup reapplied and her coat across her arm, she descended the hallway and awaited Jordan to escort her to her, probably by now, snow-covered car.

Jordan waited for her in the lounge, practically counting the minutes to see the absolutely intoxicating Eve Harlan again. He looked at the young woman approaching him but could hardly believe she was the same mermaid he had made love to only an hour ago. He didn't know it was possible for her to look even better than she already did, but when she stopped directly in front of him, he saw that same beautiful face with the pouty lips and dazzling light brown eyes. He took her hands into his. "Well, look at you. I must say you look so super sexy, but I liked you in the swimsuit better. I could see more flesh, and it tasted incredible."

Eve had the same reaction when seeing him out of tight-fitting trunks; he was different but the same, dressed in a dark blue suit with a stark white dress shirt underneath. He looked pristine, almost sparkling. She liked his new look; it made him look like the professor he was, but with an incredibly sexy flair. With his hair combed and dried, she could see exactly how sensual he was. The first thing she did was run her fingers through his golden locks, letting the silky strands tickle her fingers. "It feels just as good dry as it does wet. One thing I'd change, though—you should lose the suit. Don't get me wrong; you look sexy as the dickens in it, but it's a shame to cover those muscles."

"You want me to catch my death out there in the middle of winter wearing only trunks?"

"We can save the trunks for the privacy of the pool again next Thursday evening."

"Or my house."

His abruptness startled her, making her answer slowly. "We . . . maybe one day soon."

"Very soon, I hope, Ms. Harlan. Do you have anyone to rush home to?"

"Not at the moment, but there's always case files to go over for tomorrow morning's meeting."

"Sounds boring. What do you do?"

"I'm a case manager for Blue Cross and Blue Shield."

"Those files can wait a few more minutes, can't they? Long enough to grab some coffee?"

Eve was certainly tempted to go anywhere with him, especially since he looked so scrumptious in that suit. The only thing she'd end up doing while in his company was dream about shedding that suit and getting down again with him. She wouldn't get in her own bed until after midnight. Being sleepy and facing other managers at nine in the morning wouldn't work. "No, I'd better get home. Long day ahead of me tomorrow."

"Another time then?"

"I'd love that."

He slid her coat over her shoulders and arms, put his own on, and took her hand. "Where are you parked?"

"The structure on Warren."

"Good, that's next to the faculty one. Let's get moving before the snow hits. We're expecting another three inches before it's all said and done."

They walked together in the dark snowy night, getting to know each other, finding out major and minor things about each other's family. Eve discovered that he was the youngest of two boys, lived in St. Claire Shores, and had been teaching at Wayne State since graduating from Princeton eleven years before with a doctorate in language arts.

He discovered that she was a maniac for dance clubs, nights home alone, and the company of the right man. He knew already that he wanted to be that *right man*. To Jordan, however, nothing mattered but being with her. It could have been a blizzard outside but he'd have seen only Eve, and everything in her garden. What he ultimately found out was that she was an only child, a graduate of the University of Michigan

with a master's in business administration, and the prettiest
damn thing he'd ever seen in his life. What he also discovered
was that he was more attracted to her than he had been to
any woman, black or white. She was a must in his boring life,
and he had to trap her—if she'd let him.

He escorted her to her Benz, kissed her lips once more, and
waited as she started the car. It didn't start. She tried again as
he waited—still nothing. She poked her head through the
window. "I don't know what's wrong with it. It started fine
today, and it's only two months old."

"Pop the hood. I don't know much about cars, but I can
take a look."

"Are you sure?"

"Positive."

Eve did as told and got out, looking at something she had
no idea about, it was nothing but pumps, hoses, wires, and
other weird-looking instruments. She bent in closer, barely
inches from the engine and, of course, from Jordan, smelling
his cologne, something cool and crisp, halfway taking her
mind from her stubborn Mercedes. "What do you think is
wrong with it?"

"I haven't the vaguest idea, to tell you the truth. All I do is
replace batteries and an occasional fuse. Other than that, I
don't know." He looked at his watch. "Do you have an emer-
gency towing service you can call?"

"Not really. I could call the motorist club, but they take
forever, and on a night like tonight, it would take longer."

"You're right."

"I'm just stuck."

"I'll take you home, sweetheart. You can't think I'd leave
you here." He took her cold hands into his, blowing on them
briefly. "Let's make sure she's all locked up, then we can go.
You can call someone in the morning."

"I hate to leave it here. I just got it, and I've wanted this
car my entire life."

Jordan took his cell out. "Let me see if my towing company will come. Sometimes Julian keeps late hours. Let's hope he does tonight."

Eve watched as Jordan made his call. Within seconds, he was making plans with Julian and giving directions. "What's your address, Eve? He may have to tow it to your house until you can get it fixed in the morning."

"Really? Christ! 203 Baltimore between Hamilton and Second." She listened until he clicked off. "Well, what's the verdict?"

"Some good news, some bad. The good—Julian can come and get it."

"And the bad news?"

"He can't come until one a.m."

"One? What am I supposed to do?"

"Go and get coffee with me. I'll stay with you, Eve, as long as you want me to."

Her shoulders slumped, her purse trudging across her knees, she said, "Well, coffee on a night like this does sound good."

"I've got a good place we can go; best damn coffee on the face of the earth."

"Where would that be?"

"My house. I roast my own coffee, grind my own beans, and I have all flavors. Are you game for the best coffee of your life?"

"If you grind beans as good as you ground me, I'm in for a hell of a French roast."

"You sure are, and I promise to be a good boy and leave you alone—unless you tell me otherwise."

"We'll see how the evening goes."

"And, if you like, I'll take you home once the car arrives."

"Again, we'll see. That might be pretty late."

"You're worth staying up all night for." He looked at his pants. "In fact, I'm up right now, and take my word for it, it's not the cold doing this."

Eve shook her head, noticing that damn fine erection. "Jordan, you're a heck of a dude."

Once inside Jordan's car, he made sure she fastened her seatbelt, and then he did his, before reaching over and kissing her with power and force, almost as though he felt he'd never see her again.

Within all that cold, Eve's lips were the warmest things he'd ever tasted, and so succulent. He almost couldn't control himself, taking her belt off and pressing her quilted body against his. "Even through all those layers of wool, I can feel your heat, Eve, and it's about to burn me up."

"Then it isn't just me feeling like a fiery pit. One more of those kisses, Jordan, and we'll be responsible for torching this parking structure."

He took one last nibble on her delectable lips, then regretfully replaced her belt. "Imagine that, student and professor torch campus parking structure; details at eleven. Let's hit the street so we can burn up private property, mine and yours."

With the snow hitting the windshield of his sky-blue Chrysler convertible, with top definitely up, he cleared it away with the wipers as they exited onto the main street leading to the freeway. At a red light, Jordan again took advantage of a few seconds and kissed her again, feeling her warm lips quickly reheating his. He slowly pulled away. "I'm sorry about your car."

"So am I, but it's been a great evening. I don't know what I'd have done without you."

"I hate to think of it. Out here alone and in the cold; an easy target for a sex-crazed man like me."

A verbal response wasn't good enough. Her hands moved between his legs and rubbed the warmth of his crotch, making it hard and spicy again. "You're not sex-crazed, just sexually gifted."

"I'd love to do more, and get more."

He turned onto Eight Mile Road after a long stretch of I-94

and headed for his home in St. Claire Shores, making time so he could be with a special lady in the privacy of his own home.

Once Eve realized what street she was on, she stared out at the night sky, passing mansion after mansion, getting glimpses of sparkling Lake St. Claire behind each home. It glistened wildly as the gentle night air tossed the waves about. Dotted lights from the lighthouse cascaded across the rippling water, making it seem that much more magical. "Do you live in one of those?" she asked, pointing to a passing mansion.

"Sure do."

"You mentioned Detroit's east side, but I didn't know it was this far east. This is the millionaire district."

"It does cost a piece to live here." He pulled into his circular drive. "This is an old family home. My parents moved out years ago and asked me if I wanted it. I grew up here, so certainly I said sure. I fixed it up my way, and now it's a real home, with all my wants and desires in it. Once you're inside, I'll have it all."

Eve stared up at the looming house that had a single light speckling a corner window. From what she could see of his property, it was extremely manicured. Freshly plowed snowblower tracks traced his walkway and sidewalks. The finely trimmed bushes had a dusting of snow across them.

The air was so calm, the surroundings so quiet, other than the waves hitting the coastline. She took Jordan's arm. "This is so gorgeous. I've always wanted to see the inside of one of these places."

"Tonight's your night, then."

"You may not be able to drag me away from it. A delicious guy and a mansion—that's a girl's dream come true."

"I may not let you leave, Mercedes or not! Come on, let's get started on that coffee. I even have whipped cream."

She smiled proudly at him. "Jordan, you're all right, and so is that bulge in your pants."

"There's more where that came from, sweetheart."

When they stepped inside, Eve's eyes widened at the immaculacy as Jordan turned on a dim light in the living room. The hardwood floors cast a gloss across everything, as if it were covered with clear water. The twenties-style furniture looked untouched. Everything was in place, unblemished. She slowly walked around the furniture, lightly touching it as Jordan looked on. Everything she touched felt rich, easy, from another lifetime, a quiet kind of eerie time, as though she were reliving the movie *The Ghost and Mrs. Muir.*

She caught a glimpse of Jordan watching her as she enjoyed her tour. "This is fabulous. I'm almost afraid to touch anything."

"Baby, you can touch everything. Toss it about if you like."

"It's too beautiful to take out of perspective. You said you grew up here?"

"Sure did. Many moons ago."

Eve made a half-turn in the middle of the room, lifting her arms in glee to the high ceiling. "I can almost hear two little golden-haired boys enjoying a Christmas filled with toys and love, right here in the middle of this room." She pointed to a corner. "Was the tree here?"

"When we had one."

She didn't expect that response. "Loving households always have a tree."

"Sure, loving ones."

She approached him, fingering the lapels of his tailored coat, staring at his face as the dim light barely shone against it in shadows. "Weren't you a happy little boy in this great big beautiful house?"

"Houses don't necessarily make the family."

Her hand tenderly grazed his cheek, feeling the tension in his face so suddenly. "Jordan? What was it—

His demeanor suddenly changed, along with his topic of conversation. "You know, there's an entire floor in this house that is simply magical. That's where I stay most of the time. Wanna see it?"

Eve bore witness to the sudden change of topic. Something happened in this ghost of a house; something that made little boys want to hurry and grow up—particularly one little boy. She lightened her composure, suddenly needing to make him happy again. "Sure, I'd love to see it."

"Great. I have a kitchen up there." He winked. "The coffee beans are also up there."

"And I can smell them already."

He kissed her neck while sliding the coat from her willing body. "There's also a view of that magnificent lake that's breathtaking. When my mind gets heavy from life, that's where I go. It's so incredible in winter. You get to see the snow cascading down, blending in with the rest of the water. The moon is so full in winter, casting such a shine on the water. Tonight is one of those nights, Eve."

She slid his coat from him, running her hands up and down his chest, feeling taut muscles aching to be caressed again. Her voice a bit raspy, she said, "Let's get up there. Hell, between you and that moon, I may forget about the coffee."

"Or the Mercedes?"

"Do you want me to forget it?"

"Tonight, nothing exists but you and I. If that's possible."

"It is."

They ascended the winding staircase hand in hand. Jordan couldn't remember the last time he brought a woman here, letting her explore the one place he could call his. No other woman was ever privileged to know so much about Jordan or had ever had access to his crystal palace by the lake.

Once they reached the top of the staircase, Eve looked around in amazement at the large technocrystal chandelier and endless hallway dotted with door after door of rooms. And on each wall, contemporary paintings by Georgia O'Keeffe, Jasper Johns, Romare Bearden, and all the greats. Art was Eve's downfall—along with sweet, gorgeous men. She automatically went to the O'Keeffe study of Lake George by moonlight, her eyes dazzled by the sensual strength of it. "This is gorgeous. You really love the water, don't you?"

Jordan moved in behind her, tenderly nibbling her earlobe. "Almost as much as I adore you. To answer your question, yes, I love the water; always have ever since I was three years old. Maybe that's why I'm a part-time swim instructor." He chuckled against her warm neck. "Well, that and the fact that I knew I'd meet the perfect lady in the water one day."

"You knew that? A premonition maybe?"

"No. A fact. Look who's in my arms tonight."

She faced him. "I guess the water does have some perks."

With their faces barely apart, he agreed. "More perks than I could have ever imagined."

"You were three years old when you learned to swim? Who taught you? Your dad?"

His demeanor suddenly changed. "Yeah, dear old dad."

"He must be a terrific swimmer himself to have taught a baby."

"You know, speaking of water, this painting is nothing compared to what's in my favorite room. Come on, you'll love this."

Eve gladly tagged behind him, just glad to have the opportunity to view a palace like this. She'd never been in one of those mansions, though she'd passed by them many times. She didn't grow up poor—just your average middle-class home in the heart of Detroit's West Side; nothing as grand as this. What made it better was being with a man like Jordan, handsome beyond reality, seemingly as rich as the Rockefellers, but only one problem, his constant avoidance of his father. That did concern Eve, and she had always been the type to do a little investigating, but with Jordan, she'd have to wait on that so as not to scare him off with questions. She knew the fastest way to turn a man off was to persist on topics they were touchy about.

Jordan opened one of the many bedroom doors and held it

out for her. At first, all she could see was a large dark room until he walked inside and turned on a faint lamp sitting on an end table. To her amazement, the first thing to greet her was a window that spanned the length of the room. She slowly walked to it, seeing the perfect full moon, seemingly large enough to see from another galaxy. Below the sky were miles and miles of lake. It was breathtaking, and Eve was breathless at the sight of it. Her whisper-soft voice cracked a bit. "No wonder this is your favorite place. Look at that lake."

"I told you it was amazing. This room by itself is the reason I'll probably never sell this house."

"Who could blame you? This is spectacular, Jordan. You can see everything, every star in the sky, every wave and ship in the water."

"Doesn't it look incredible with the faint lighting from the lamp? Soft light cascading from a view like this makes this room seem so magical."

Eve continued to stare in wonder of the view. "Awesome. I'll bet you spend a lot of time in here."

"Every chance I get. I do everything in here—lesson plans, computer stuff—but usually at the end of a long day, I'll come in here and max out with a glass of wine, think about my day, my dreams, my schemes."

"You know what that sounds like?"

"What? Someone who's self-absorbed?"

"Not at all. It reminds me of a Brian Wilson song, "In My Room.""

"I know that one, and it's so true, Eve. I really do my dreaming and scheming in here. I can tell my secrets out loud and no one but me can hear them." He took her hand, kissing her soft, long fingers. "I'm dreaming right now. It's not every night I have a lovely young woman at my side—in my room."

Eve turned to him again, so enthralled with his sensitive words. "I love how you talk to me. I've never been so captivated with a man I just met a few hours ago. You've brought out something in me, Jordan. You make me wild, brave. You make me feel beautiful, in mind and body."

"You are that, and in every way a woman can be. And being in here, in the dark, watching the snow drift into the water and highlighted by that dazzling full moon, well, nothing's been more perfect in my life."

Eve etched a sensual kiss on his waiting lips, taking him in, loving this night, loving that window—loving him, if only for the moment. His body felt so strong in her arms, yet his sensitive side was just as enthralling. Jordan was a delicious jock of a man who swam in the water with grace and style. However, the enormous bulge in his pants made her well aware that he was now dressed in a business suit she was anxious to take off. Remembering how his body felt against and inside of her made her yearn for him like no other man in her life.

Jordan moved his hands up and down the wool of her business suit, slid the jacket off, and stroked her body through the silk blouse. His lips barely moved from hers. "I'd better get that damn coffee made or we'll never get it. I'm content to stay right here with you, Eve, in this moment, in this lifetime."

"We don't have to have the coffee. We can just stay here by this lovely window and dream dreams together."

"I can't just talk to you, Eve. You're too amazing not to touch. But I know how warm you really are. As in hot. You torched my erection so well that I'm still smoking from you. I plan to burn all night, if you'll let me."

"I'll let you, all right. I'll let you do anything your dear heart desires because I'm a willing participant."

"Good. Then you stay here. I have all kinds of wonderful imported coffees, teas, wines, even hot chocolate. What's your desire?"

She ran her finger down the length of his chest, stopping to dip a finger into the dent of his shirt, touching his navel with sultry strokes. "I love white chocolate, and I know you have plenty of that. I want enough to satisfy me all night, Jordan. Can you handle that?"

A smile lit up his face, making him forget everything but the woman before him. "Definitely."

Eve stroked the front of his dress pants, feeling the length she was so hot for that she could barely stand not having him inside her. "Whatever you're about to make in that kitchen, do it in a hurry. Nothing would be more perfect than seeing the moon shine down on the prettiest man I've ever seen."

He started unbuttoning his shirt, showing her hints of everything to come. Once the shirt was fully open, exposing his perfectly toned chest, his hand moved up and down it, giving himself goose bumps from imagining her hands there. "Give me a few minutes. What I have for you the rest of this night will simply intoxicate both of us—again." One more kiss against her lips, then he was off.

Eve watched him walk from the room and stared at the door for seconds, relishing the idea of Jordan Whittaker. She briefly returned to the splendor of the water view, then discovered that the rest of the large room housed a leather sofa, a large-screen television, a state-of-the-art computer, and a bookshelf full of books.

Eve was an avid reader and loved all kinds of books. She was curious about his taste in literature. Mystery and suspense dominated. While pulling one of the many Edgar Allan Poe books from the shelf, her foot nudged something in the corner. She quickly pulled on the item until it gave way. It was a painting of a man. She held it up near the faint lamp, noticing the man looked an awful lot like Jordan. *Is this his father?*

Eve continued to stare at the gorgeous man in the painting. His eyes were like Jordan's, and he had the same golden hair, but worn combed back. Still, he was incredibly handsome in his gray business suit. It was the kind of painting one would see on the walls of an overly expensive restaurant at Somerset

Mall, a regular captain-of-industry-type painting. *Then what was the deal with Jordan being so close-mouthed about his father?*

Eve replaced the painting, but kept a leather-bound copy of *The Raven* tucked under her arm to borrow from him. She loved Poe's books and the many movies based on them. It was a good night for reading a mystery—but a better night for making love. She retreated back to the window, staring at how the winds were picking up, making the water ripple almost out of control. Had she not been with a man she trusted, the scenario would have been rather eerie: dark waves crushing against the shore, a lighthouse in the distance blinking in isolation, an old painting of a man who apparently had a sordid past and a very, very still house. The only difference, it was a modern mansion, not a set from a Vincent Price movie, and the owner was definitely not spooky. However, her quick and unyielding attraction to him was.

As she stared through the window, thinking of nothing but Jordan, she began to smell delicious aromas coming from the kitchen. Definitely a hazelnut roast, one with a kick, but a kick of what, she didn't know.

Minutes later, Jordan came back in with a tray that contained two miniature mugs of steaming hot liquid with cinnamon sticks poking from the tops and a few tea biscuits. He sat the tray on the table near her and took her hand. "Are you ready for something really toasty? Something that is so toasty that it'll take your mind from that big old window?"

"That happened the minute you walked into the room, my dear."

"I made us something sweeter than me. I have a bitter aftertaste once you get to know me."

"I doubt that. Maybe you haven't been around the right people."

"Perhaps not, but tonight is different."

He led her to the sofa and handed her the steaming drink. "You said you like white chocolate, so I made us a hazelnut roast with a bit of coconut liquor in it. Does that sound appetizing?"

"That wasn't exactly the white chocolate I had in mind, but yes, it sounds wonderful."

"Well, at least this will take your mind from your Mercedes."

"I don't need liquor to do that. That's a first, since I love that car so much."

"I'm sure it'll be ready for you in the morning." He looked at his watch and smiled back at her. "We have plenty of time before morning. Besides, we have so much still to do."

Eve took a sip from her mug. "Umm, this is delicious; almost as delicious as my treat earlier this evening. Which brings me to what you just said."

"Which was?"

"You said we have a lot to do this evening. What would you like to do?"

He took a long sip from his coffee, thought about the possibilities the evening could bring, then placed the coffee on the table. "I'd love to resume what we were doing in the shower. I've never done it there . . . well, not like that. I've made love to women in many places, but it seemed to mean more with you. But there are other things. We could talk, watch movies, anything your heart desires."

"Cuddling. Talking and cuddling. I'd really like to know who Jordan Whittaker really is other than that delicious hunk of burnin' love I had incredible sex with only hours ago. I know there's more to you, Jordan, than swimming, this house, and the fact that you teach at a major university."

"There is, but I'm boring. Why don't we start with you? You're the one with personality in every cell of your body."

"Hardly!"

"I'm serious, Eve. You asked me how I knew your name out of a pool of women. I told you only someone like you could look so sensual. The real Eve was supposed to be sensual, and, baby, you live up to the name. She just about drove

Adam crazy if I'm not mistaken. Besides, the minute I looked at you, I knew you were the one."

"The one?"

He moved in closer, still able to smell a mixture of her pheromone perfume and the incredible sex they had shared. Her scent almost made him lose track of reality. "Yes, the only one. I've never seen a beauty like you before."

That was the single most touching thing a man had ever said to her and it tugged at her heartstrings. She traced a hand along his jaw. "That's the sweetest thing I've ever heard come from a man."

"Then you've been around the wrong men."

"That's quite possibly true, but I'm just still surprised that my fear of water didn't turn you off."

He tugged at the strap of her red lace shell, lowering it from her shoulder. The feel of her skin against his lips made him warmer than any coffee he could have brewed that evening. "Nothing Eve Harlan could do would turn me off."

Eve leaned against him, feeling his half-exposed chest against her hair and hands, feeling it vibrate as he spoke. Her fingers delicately roamed his pecs, circling his nipples, then trailing down. She loved how he felt, how he smelled. Jordan smelled rich but not overpowering, not rich enough to look over the world from his own cloud. No, Jordan was real, earthy, very male, but with a child still housed within his heart. Despite that, she wanted him, needed to be in his life somehow.

His voice delivered her from her temporary flight to heaven. "What made you want to learn to swim, other than your trip? I know it has to be something else."

"There are two something else's. I wanna look like a pro in the water, let everyone know that a Michigan girl can play with more toys than snowmobiles and skis. I want to be able to say that I learned how to swim in Detroit—the last place anyone would think about learning to swim."

"And the other reason?"

Eve didn't want to dredge up memories of almost drowning. She feared he'd take pity on her, treat her like a delicate crystal while in the water. She didn't want that. Eve needed to get rid of that fear for her own sake, mostly, not simply to look good in a pool. "My father is a wonderful man, Jordan."

That took him by surprise. He hadn't expected to hear about her father out of nowhere. "I'm . . . I'm sure he is to have a daughter like you. But what does that have to do with—

"My father saved me, Jordan. I almost drowned in a pool when I was seven years old. I was playing around, trying to prove to everyone that I could teach myself to swim. When everyone went inside, I got back into my aunt's pool and went out a little too far. When I couldn't reach the bottom, I panicked, fought the water, swallowed more than I could handle and was on my way down." She relaxed in his arms, for once feeling OK with telling her frightening tale. "The funny thing is, I remember looking through the water and seeing my father dive in. He took care of me that day, held me, comforted me. Everyone came to my side, but all I wanted was my father." She looked up at Jordan with a contented smile on her face. "I still need my father so much, but he's not the only one anymore."

"Am I in that esteemed group?"

"Can't you see how I'm looking at you?"

He kissed her forehead. "The minute I looked at you, I figured it would be impossible to be in your life, Eve."

"Why?"

"You looked too good for me."

"Don't say things like that. You're perfect, warm, gentle, caring—everything I love in a man." She stared into his eyes. "What would make you say something like that about yourself?"

"My past relationships."

Eve knew it was more but assumed he was reluctant to tell. She had to know, though, drag it out of him and learn who she was really with. As usual she went about it the complex way. "When did your dad teach you how to swim?"

"I can't really remember. I think I was born swimming. Actually, I take that back. I was three and a half when my parents took my brother and me to Turtle Bay. I remember being excited about going so I could find turtles. Instead, I learned the backstroke. Dad said I was a natural . . ."

His words trailed, taking Eve by surprise. "Why did you stop?"

"Eve, talking about my father— it just isn't the best topic for me."

"Why? What happened to you? You can tell me, Jordan, and it will stay in this room. I promise."

"It's not you that concerns me. You're the best part of my life, and I found you in one evening, but my childhood wasn't grand. I don't even think I believe in childhood anymore."

That took her, softened her heart in regards to him, making her want to soothe the rough edges that apparently were created by people who shouldn't have been parents. She took his hand in hers and leaned farther into his warm chest. "What happened in your life to make you say that?"

"My father was hardly around. You know, always on business trips, closing deals, making new ones. When he was home, he was never really there. He'd sit in his study and ignore my mother and us boys. He was cool when we were younger, but when we got some age on us, able to make up our own minds and think for ourselves, all hell broke loose. With me, it was especially hard." His hands moved up Eve's shell, caressing satin skin, wanting to touch her in ways he had only experienced with her. But he knew Eve was inquisitive and would demand he finish what he started. "It was harder with me because I was a dreamer, wanted to be a surfer, stuff like that. My brother is hard-nosed, realistic, and that's good for him but not for me. I marched to my own drummer and that royally ticked off the important Franklyn

Whittaker. I was accepted on the Olympic team at age six-teen, but my father said no. He taught me to swim in the first place; then he took it all away."

"That's a great accomplishment, Jordan. Getting accepted on the Olympic team is an honor. But maybe your father wanted you to do something that would last you a lifetime."

"I thought that was it also, but nothing I liked doing was right for him. I wanted to practice criminal law, working in the inner city, but he wouldn't go for it. I liked social work, but he said no son of his would do meaningless work like that. Finally, I decided to do my own thing—teach literature. That got his goat, too, but at that point, I didn't care. Hell, it was my life."

Spoken like a real man, Eve thought. All he'd wanted to do was the right thing, despite his controlling father. "You're a big sweetheart, aren't you?"

"I wanna be."

"You are. You have a good heart, Jordan. As rich as you and your family are, you still wanted to work with less fortu-nate people. Only a really good man could or would want to do that. Working with the general public and in impover-ished neighborhoods isn't easy."

"But important."

"Exactly. And something in those big beautiful eyes told me you were special."

"Flawed."

"Aren't we all?"

"Not you, and what's important right now, Ms. Harlan, is taking you to my bedroom and making love to you until we both pass out. No more talk of fathers, swimming, sad little boys, or anything like that. Tonight belongs to me for once, and I see everything I want wrapped up in a delicious brown package."

"Would your father dislike the brown part?"

"Most definitely, but don't worry, he lives in Boca Raton

with my mother, who still trails him around like a little pet. She was the only sweet part of my childhood."

"Mothers are supposed to love their little boys, especially sweet ones like I know you were. Do you think she'd like me?"

"She'd adore you. Eve, she adores anything that makes Joseph and me happy."

"Your brother is named Joseph?"

"Yes, another great person. He lives here but in the upper peninsula."

She took another slow sip from her coffee, then returned to him. "Can I ask you something?"

"Anything you like. You know that, beautiful."

"Don't take this the wrong way, but do you like me simply because your father wouldn't?"

"Eve, despite how he tried controlling my life, there are some things he could never have control over, such as my women. I'm crazy about you, and that's all that matters to me. Your complexion is part of who you are, and I love who that is."

"Have you ever dated an African American woman?"

He relaxed against the sofa. "Once, years ago."

"What happened?"

"Graduation. She went her way and I went mine. We weren't meant to be together, but times have changed since then." Jordan finished the last of his coffee, took her hand in his and kissed it. "Now, if you don't mind, I'd love to show you the view from my other favorite room, and there's an added feature—a king-sized bed made only for a queen." He laid her half-finished glass mug on the coffee table and hoisted her petite, slender frame into his arms. "Ready to make love again for the third time?"

His emerald eyes sparkled against the moon from the window, giving him a sexier than possible aura. "I think you're the only thing in my life that I am ready for. I want you to make true and total love to me, Jordan, and let me do the same to you. I wanna be wild with you, hungry, crazy, self-ish—everything I can be with you. No holds barred, Mr. Jordan."

"Then come along and kill me with it."

They didn't even bother to turn down the bedsheets. All they needed to undress each other was the dim moonlight cascading once again from another large window. Eve could hardly wait to remove everything from him and witness perfection again. He was the like the statue of David, but with an erection that would make that noted work of art look small.

Undressing him was a feast, starting with the few buttons remaining closed on his dress shirt. Each bit of skin she uncovered was met with a lavish lick and a tender kiss. The feel of his warm, wet nipples against her tongue ignited something within her that was unmet before. Wildness took over her mind and soul. She'd had Jordan inside of her twice since six that evening, but something was different this time.

As she kissed and stroked his nipples, and trailed her fingertips down his chest and stomach, she realized what the difference was—the atmosphere. It was romantic this time, peaceful, still, just right for perfect lovemaking. That, coupled with the anticipation of making intense love to a man she could never get her fill of, was controlling her thought processes. Jordan was the most beautiful man she had ever seen, that was all there was to it.

As she slowly lowered his zipper, she could feel him watching her, delicious green eyes so piercing and intense that he could probably see her thoughts. His words did nothing but develop an already intense situation. "Take me, Eve. Take me into your garden and let me fulfill your wildest dreams."

His engorged phallus seemed to have gotten hotter and stiffer. She helped him out of his pants, leaving a crumpled heap of cloth in the middle of his floor, and took him. She was suddenly so insatiably hungry for him. He was so adoring, so sweet, and that was the real attraction. All that sweetness belonging to someone so real.

She moved lower, letting him guide his shaft deeper and deeper into her longing throat. He rocked slowly at first, letting her suck and devour him at her own pace. He watched as his darling Eve took on more and more, building her speed, latching on to him, pulling and milking him in ways that made him want immediate release. But it was too good to be over without pleasing her to the max. He let her get her fill, caressing his shaft, sucking his tip, dipping her tongue into places that needed ultimate attention. His hand joined hers, stroking it, teasing her lips with it, stroking her cheeks and feeling his meat inside her mouth.

His shirt dropped to the carpet, and Eve's hand immediately reached up to stroke strong, hard pecs and an abdomen as flat and hot as pancakes but with the feel of satin. She pulled from him, letting his tip slowly ride the outer edge of her lips. "I have to feel you inside me, Jordan. I'm so hot and burning—hot enough to squeeze my precious man into submission. Would you like that, baby? Do you want to be squeezed and taken so deeply that you won't return to reality for another week?"

"I want any and all things from the Garden of Eden, and that includes the best part—you." He pulled her to her feet, smelling the traces of perfume on her body. That drove him to get at her again.

His lips gingerly traced hers, darting his tongue teasingly in and out of her mouth, making her hunger for him way beyond what she had already experienced. He wanted her, needed her, and in ways he didn't want to need another woman. He had practically overdosed on women—until that night. Eve was different; she fulfilled another need he had—to be loved.

Jordan quickly kissed down her jaw line, neck, and shoulders and removed her silky shell. From that point on, her breasts were his. He took them within the palms of his hands, enjoying their warmth. Tight buds pressed against his hands, swelling, asking for more attention. He clued in immediately and took one nipple, the then other, completely into his mouth, sucking and drawing back, snapping lovingly at them, teasing them to stay hard for him. Soon his tongue spiraled down her tummy, poking into her navel while removing her skirt. The feel of her thong within his grasp aroused him even more. He looked up at her, a devilish smile erupting on his features. "The golden temple of the Himalayas is right at my beck and call, gorgeous. Shall I expose the temple again to a very determined king?"

Eve couldn't help but giggle at his words. "Where do you get these things from?"

"My favorite movie, *Brighton Beach Memoirs*. I watch a lot of movies when I'm not in the company of a fabulous young woman or giving speeches at other universities."

Her fingers made ringlets in his hair. "Go for it, king."

"As you wish." He slid the thong down her silky legs and exposed all of her. He was almost insane from wanting her. He fingered her velvety mound, seducing her folds with gentle touches. Each sinfully rich seduction made her tremble within his grasp, and her arousal showed on her face, much to his pleasure. He took it further, sliding one, then two fingers completely into her dampened sex, feeling her drenching powers, teasing her clit with expert precision.

Eve literally vibrated to his touch, crying out to him, moving into him, wanting, needing, everything that she knew Jordan could eagerly supply. She stroked his neck and shoulders with loving caresses, having never remembered touching a man so sincerely. What was it about this man? She wanted to love him, wanted to be his everything. Her voice whispered barely audible words, "I need to see you, Jordan. I need to really see you."

"I'm here, baby, and for as long as you want me." He pulled her to her knees, moved in behind her, and again showed her one of his many talents. A swift tongue lapped at her opening, smothering himself within her juices, dipping deeper and deeper into her well until he felt he'd nearly run her dry. Damn, she was so outrageously delicious! No one anywhere left that much of a lasting aroma on his mind and body, but she had, and he had to have more. The more Eve called to him, the more he ate away at her. Fingers and tongue doing double action on a beautiful queen almost took him there, so ready to spill for her, but he held back, wanting to give her the best he could possibly offer.

Jordan felt her contractions as his tongue coiled around her clit, holding him, quivering against him, aching for complete and total release. Though he hated to leave anything that juicy, he knew they both had to have it, to treat the right parts with the right friction and lose their minds in the process. Jordan was past that point with her and so ready to feel everything. He brought her face-to-face with him. "You want more, sugar?"

His shaft pressed so hard against her stomach that she could barely imagine anything other than feeling it inside her again. "I want it, Jordan. I want it so bad. I'm aching for you like you wouldn't believe." She stroked his warm cheek. "What do you do to me?"

"Everything I possibly can." At that, he lifted her into his arms and carried her to the bed, laying her against the silk sheets. He loomed above her, completely naked, staring down at naked perfection. He was speechless. Looking down at something so awesome and on his bed was beyond words. His only possible action: mount her and ascend to paradise.

Her thighs automatically parted for him, wrapping around his tight body and holding on for wild lovemaking of a lifetime. Jordan was the *only* man who could do it. They clad him with satiny protection seconds before temptation clouded both their judgment. His shaft poked at her wet sex, rubbing it, playing it to ripeness. Her anticipation grew, her wildness surfaced, and the begging began. "Don't tease me, Jordan, please."

"Do you want it bad, or do you want it good?"

"Any way; just slide deep into me, touch my soul, make my body singe from fire. Now, Jordan. Now."

At her very demand, he entered her, feeling her tight core wrap around his thick shaft, pulling him, tugging him, making him insane for her heat. He pumped soft and smooth as he filled her completely, then increased the tempo, rocking his hips in unison with hers. His tight body racked hers, pumping so hard and diligently that the room seemingly spun out of control for him. That didn't matter. What mattered was that he was looking down into the face of saving grace. He gave and gave, slowly dripping sex into the snug condom, and he stayed relentless in his efforts to give Eve everything she was crying for. He wiped the tears from her stained, glorious face and kissed her lips to his on rhythm. "Is this good, baby? Is this the best you've ever imagined? I know it is for me. Just looking down at you makes me so hard and tight, tight enough to spray out of control."

Yes, he was definitely hard enough for that. She could feel his exquisite stiffness as it continued to impale her. His veins stroked her walls, teasing them, rubbing, soothing all that scorching heat within her. Eve hadn't experienced that kind of heat and tension before, having never expected to get it from a white man. She'd believed those old, stupid stories of white men not having what it took. One look at Jordan Whittaker with the Sears Tower poking from the front of his trunks and she knew those stories were inaccurate. It was all in the man himself, not the color, and from the very sight of Jordan, she knew she had to experience his myth firsthand— a myth and a tale that only he could tell. And now that he was on top of her, not a damn thing else in the world mattered.

Jordan slowly pulled from her, placing her on her knees and moving in behind her. "You want to really make me come? All I need is this." He moved slowly into her, forcing his way back into her tight, wet core with a pushing/pulling action and keeping an even pace. Something about rear entry took him to his limits, and now that Eve was the one supplying the goods, ecstasy was just over the hill.

It was glorious. Her tight, wet mound was feverish for him, begging him to take her deeper, slam into her, ride her like a wild bronco—and he did, always following her commands to the very letter. Eve's back arched to his roughness, feeling him spread her apart. Their bodies rocked in harmony, meat against meat, vibrating, humming in perfect unity. Her hand reached between them, feeling his juices as he pumped into her, tickling the underside of the few inches of him not hidden by her sex. Her fingers rubbed him, nails tickled him, making him increase his pace, making her holler out of control. She could feel his scrotum slamming against her, gyrating in circular motions as he brought her to sexual ecstasy.

Every inch of him pressed into her as she called and screamed to him, begging him to go deeper, deeper, deeper. Jordan couldn't stand it. He leaned atop her back, his hands full of her breasts, shaking her, drilling her, moaning, thrusting. Sweet, sticky sweat dripped from him and on to her as the pressure built. Finally, that moment came . . . and so did he, over and over, spilling life into that condom, squirting in all directions, breaking the condom while riding her into blissful nothingness.

Eve felt it and cried out but God was the only name called over and over, though it was a man who thrilled her so. Jordan Whittaker, man of the hour, king of the night.

He slumped to her side, chest heaving. He looked over at her, smiling at the vision resting on the second pillow. His fingers moved dark strands from her flushed face. "I've never had anything like that before, Eve. Never. What is it about you that takes me back to the jungle?"

"Perfect lovemaking takes only two things: the right man and the right woman."

"Am I the right man?"

"If my body still aches for and from you in two days, damn straight you're the right man!"

"But what about now?"

She kissed his moist lips again, pressing her soft body into the sweaty hardness of his. "You are everything you look to be—fabulous, tight, buff, and so super sexy, Jordan. I love being here with you. Could easily make this a habit."

"Make it a habit? You're already mine. I'd have to go to rehab to shake you." He pulled the blanket over them both, moved her body into the front of his, and rested with the idea of her next to him. That was the only time Jordan had ever gone to sleep so easily, with the best of the best flush against his own wanting skin.

Two hours later, Eve awakened suddenly, looking out at the still dark, starry morning. The snow continued to drift down into the lake, the moon still so high and bright in the sky. Shadows danced across the room, and she pulled the covers over her bare shoulders. This was not her home, not her bed, not her blanket. Her eyes cast to Jordan who was sound asleep, huddled next to her. She stared at his face, touching his hair, his jaw line. Her fingers delicately touched his lips, lips she'd kissed so much that her own were still swollen. He was an enigma, perfect to look at but hard to figure out.

She moved from the bed, not able to relax, and scoured the mansion. With her glass of water from the upstairs kitchen, she went into the family room and reached for the remote to the large television. What met her hands was a leather-bound photo album. Feeling only a little guilty for being so nosy, Eve opened the book, skimmed through pictures of people she had never seen before. The next picture took her. It was a large picture of Jordan but not Jordan. The man in the picture had Jordan's face, smile, eyes; a younger image of the picture of his father that she saw earlier.

Eve turned the picture over. "Franklyn Whittaker, 1969."

She looked to the ceiling. "What's with those two? He looks like a good man." Eve knew pictures could be deceiving, and from what she'd heard of good old Mr. Whittaker Senior, that beautiful picture was a lie.

She turned the page and saw a vivid Olen Mills picture of two boys. She knew it was Jordan and his brother. Beautiful little boys, smiling like the sun was theirs for the taking, but upon further inspection, she saw that the one she knew was her lover had tears in his eyes. Despite his smile, the wet eyes were a giveaway. Something bad had happened only moments before the picture was taken. The expression in the eyes was distant, the same eyes that looked at her so lovingly.

Eve closed the book, finished her water, and slowly walked back to the bed to snuggle next to her lover, if only for a few more hours.

Eve awakened again later that morning, quickly dressed, and called for a cab. She didn't dare awaken her sleeping prince after wearing him out three times the night before. On his dresser she left a note thanking him for a wonderful time and for the sex of the century; then she awaited her cab and left. Left his life? That was the question she couldn't answer.

Content that her Mercedes was safely parked in front of her house and running in perfect condition, she sped off to work and tackled the first of several boring meetings.

Beforehand, she had been too busy to think about Jordan, but now that there was a break in her schedule, the first thing her mind drifted to was him. She adored him, loved who he was, loved how he treated her like a perfect lady. But could she deal with him? He was so different from her. His upbringing was different; his way of living was different. She was used to being around loving families, good experiences, Friday night card games, block parties, chitterlings, and fried chicken on the grill. Ordinary joys but as necessary as breathing. Could Jordan supply that for her?

Words he had spoken last night haunted her: *I don't believe in childhood*. That scared her. She was looking for a relation-ship that could take her to the ultimate goal—marriage and children. Did he want that?

Eve knew she was doing what most women do when meet-ing a fantastic man—jump to the wedding without so much as having the first date. Yet her concern was genuine. Could he handle a life with her? Eve knew she had to wait, sit back and think, be objective about the situation. If a relationship with him was in the proverbial cards, she'd let it happen nat-urally.

It had been a long day with meeting after meeting, and in between them, thoughts of her delightful Mr. Jordan contin-ued to haunt her, along with thoughts of his sheltered life. With all of that going on, she couldn't wait to get home. She hadn't been back since early the previous morning other than to change clothing. All she wanted to do was slip into a ki-mono, pour a glass of chardonnay, and put on her Aya CD, listen to "Nobody Knows Me," and veg out. The title of the soulful song once again took her back to Jordan. Did she know him? She wanted to. As she sipped her mellow wine, she remembered she had forgotten to check her answering machine. A friend of hers was due in town within the next day or two and had said she would call with specifics. Eagerly, Eve pressed the button. Yes, Bonnie would be in town, and she was glad to hear it, but it was the next message that got her.

Eve listened carefully as the seductive voice lured her. "Hello, gorgeous. It's Jordan . . . yeah, like you wouldn't have known that. I know you're wondering how I got your number, so please forgive me for getting it from your membership file at the health club. I missed seeing you this morning and wanted to tell you how incredible you are, every part of you. I'd like to see you again if that's okay with you. How's that Mercedes? My guy does a great job."

Just the sound of his voice melted her; it was so sensual,

deep, male to the max. But she still wasn't sure about anything with him yet. She jotted down his number, just in case. For that night, the only thing on tap was the rest of her glass of wine, a delicious salad, Showtime and more thoughts of Jordan no matter how much she wanted not to think of him.

The next evening after work, his clear voice was seducing her answering machine and her senses again. She had wanted to call him back the night before, revel in his sound, his words, his thoughts, but she wasn't sure what to say to him. He'd want to further their relationship, and she knew it. But how do you tell a dream man that you want to slow down?

Avoidance.

That would give her time to think.

Over the weekend, she gave nothing. He left another message. She felt bad about avoiding him, and it was getting increasingly hard, but she continued the wait, enjoying spending time with her friend and a poker game with her father and his best friend, James. The entire time, Jordan controlled her. In her own mind, she really couldn't fathom exactly *why* she was keeping her distance from a man she knew she wanted. But for Eve, it wouldn't work unless she had all of him and on her own terms.

Thursday evening came along, an evening she was dreading because she *had* to see him. She had three more weeks of swim class in order to look good in the Bahamas. She wanted to either chicken out and simply not go, or change facilities, but that wouldn't solve the problem.

By 7:30, the other women and Jordan were in the pool, awaiting the last student. No sign of Eve. He had to start class but didn't want to without her. He checked the wall clock again in case his eyes were playing games and there was still time for her to appear, but everything was right on schedule. He had messed up, done something wrong, said something crass—but what? He got it together enough to begin his class for those who were serious about swimming, and not for those serious about avoidance.

Jordan knew his students were ready to kick off the side from the deeper end. He gathered everyone and helped them tread out farther. The opening door caught his attention, and to his delight, it was the one woman he prayed he'd see again—Eve. She was the best thing he'd ever seen, better than how she looked last week. Her swimsuit fit better, sexier; her bronze skin really glowed. His happiness showed in his smile as he met her at the shallow end and reached out to take her hand. "Ms. Harlan, I was beginning to think you dropped me. I'm glad you didn't."

"I almost did."

"Why?"

Not wanting to give him the real answer, she stalled. "Still scared of water, and I'm not sure if looking like an expert in the Bahamas is worth it."

"Worth what? The jam you're in with me?"

"I'm not in a jam with you, Jordan."

"I think you are, but if you like, we can simply concentrate on the lessons and nothing more. Would that be better?"

She knew she'd hurt him by not responding to his phone calls. That was the last thing she wanted to do, and the minute she saw him, all she had wanted to do was go deep with him again, taste his wonderful lips, stroke that erection that was starting just by her arrival. She smiled coyly. "Can we maybe go slower?"

He had to play along if he wanted her in his life. "I know I move fast, Eve, but with you it's impossible to hold back. For you, I'll try. I don't want to, but I will." He led her into the middle of the pool. "We're going a little deeper. Do you want to try it?"

"Will you hold me?"

"You know I will, and I won't let go until you tell me to."

She understood his message.

Jordan held her tight as they made their way to the six-foot mark. He could tell she was scared.

Eve was *totally* scared, but willed herself to keep going. Reliving their night of unbridled love and ultimate sex was what she needed, temporarily, to take her mind from the cold water, water that could swallow her up and conceal the fact that she was ever there. There was no father to jump in and save her, just Jordan, who would gladly do the same thing. For the first time, not even Jordan, who had managed to take her mind from everything, could deliver her from the fear of the deep. She stiffened within his clutch, remembering that stifling feeling of being weighted down, seeing bubbles escape her own mouth and not be able to do a damn thing about it.

Her hands gripped the edge of the pool tighter and stayed there despite how her lover edged her on. She could see the others on the opposite side staring, waiting for her to get over there so they could continue their lesson. Eve didn't care. That mind-blowing experience twenty years ago still haunted her. "I . . . I can't do this, Jordan. I'm scared."

"I know you're scared, but I won't let go. Trust me. You trust me, don't you?"

Her jaw quivered, chilling her entire frame. "I do trust you, but I can't touch the bottom."

"You don't have to. I've got you." He did something that he normally never did—get in too close with his emotions during class. His lips moved to her wet ear, tangling with her long strands. "I'm here, baby, and I will never let anything hurt you. Please trust me. Trust me with everything." His arm wrapped tighter around her waist and edged her on.

Slowly she loosened her grip of the edge, making a move inch by inch until she, Jordan, and the rest of the class were again a team. He stayed with her, but close enough to his other, more secure students and continued to familiarize them with not touching the bottom. There were hardly any words between her and Jordan. She followed his instructions to the letter in fear of him going back on his word, but she knew within her soul that he never would.

Eve was the last to leave class, wanting to talk to Jordan about her dilemma, but she knew he'd only try to convince her that it didn't matter. As she exited the water, leaving him behind to wonder what the sudden problem was, she felt bad. Eve knew he needed reasons, but the pool wasn't the place to explain. Another day, another time. It would be a long week until she saw him again. She hoped that if she prayed hard enough, the whole situation would work itself out and she could have her perfect man. Ultimately, she knew life simply didn't operate that way.

Eve resisted responding to Jordan's calls, but by Saturday afternoon, his calls stopped. She had expected him to call late that night or Sunday, but it never came, and she missed hearing his voice on the answering machine, wondering about her, asking to see her. He was still interested after her little display of nonchalance. What was really working on her nerves was herself. She knew she was still hot for Jordan. The moment she looked at him in the pool the Thursday before, her body ached for his to be inside of hers, for his loving words to tingle her ears, for the feel of his hands on her.

Who did she think she was fooling? Jordan had infiltrated her, sautéed her emotions, and was ready to serve her over a hot, steaming plate of sexual adventures, and she wanted it— badly. She had to admit that the very idea of him, flaws and all, was more than enough. He was destined to be with her, and there was no more denying it.

After grabbing her gumption and praying that he'd want to speak to her after giving him a cold, wet shoulder, she sped to the university, found State Hall, and headed for his room.

She could hear his voice before approaching room 313. He sounded so professional, direct and to the point. He knew exactly what he was talking about, made his subject come alive as he discussed Chaucer with a group of freshmen. He knew his stuff; he was as lusty and as lively as the old English poet.

Before opening the door, she looked inside and saw him pace his room with enthusiasm, getting his students excited about learning. She also saw many a female student staring at him in awe because that's what he was—awe-inspiring, magnetic, radiating sexual energy. Eve was staring through the glass as though she were a child in the window of a candy shop. Eye candy. That would be Jordan Whittaker.

He looked so sexy in his black dress slacks and light cream shirt with the tie loosened. The way he listened to his students with his hands barely resting on his slender hips turbocharged her sex drive. She had to have him; no more thoughts, rules, apprehensions—all but one: taking it slower with him and building a relationship, if that was still attainable.

Eve quietly opened the door, and Jordan's eyes met hers. It took everything she had not to stare at him in the middle of a crowded classroom. She edged her way to the back and quickly sat down.

Jordan's eyes danced with pleasure as he watched her move down the aisle. She was there for a reason, and thank God it was for him. With a grin that wouldn't quit on his face, he finished the last twenty minutes of his class, handed out the next assignment, and patiently waited for the last student to leave.

Women came up to his desk after class all the time, obviously, and Eve knew why. They were smitten, as was she. She watched as the women sashayed around him, asking their obvious questions and doing everything humanly possible to truly nail him, but it wasn't working. His eyes continuously darted to the garden party he was being invited to. Politeness to his students lasted only so long before he whisked them off to "professor anybody but him" and walked Eve's way.

Breathless inches apart were they, with smiling faces, loving faces, insane-about-one-another faces. Jordan took her hand. "Visiting me in the middle of the day? What brought this on?"

"I wanted to see you."

He sat on the corner of the desk, hands still covering hers. "You wanted to see me, huh?" His eyes narrowed in a playful look. "Is this good or bad? You were pretty standoffish at the pool the other evening. I thought my goose was cooked when it came to you."

"Not in the least. I'm here today because I just had to see you, Jordan. I haven't been able to take my mind from you the second I met you."

"Really? I was beginning to think otherwise, with you not returning my calls, and coming late to swim class. You were giving me a complex, little lady."

She moved in closer to him, so close she could smell his cologne, wanting it to intoxicate her, lose all sense of reality. That was easy with him. She had to remember herself suddenly, remember why she was there and not get trapped by desire so quickly that she'd undo everything her sane mind was telling her. "I know I've been standoffish lately, and that's why I'm here. I need to apologize."

He stood, taking her into the crook of his arm. "No need for that. I knew something was up and that you'd tell me all about it if you wanted to. I still have that complex, though, and if you don't kiss me, it'll only get worse. Don't wear me down, Eve, because I'm already so weak for you. Just one kiss, one nibble, and I promise I'll go away."

"I don't want you to go away, Jordan, and don't beg me. You know my lips are yours, everything on me is yours." She moved into him, wrapping her arms tightly around his neck and shoulders, feeling his muscles contracting to her. Her lips softly brushed against his, feeling his velvet flesh, his warmth, the small poke of a tongue, then more, and more.

Again, he had possessed her. One touch from him and she

was so willing to give in. Her lips covered his over and over, like a game to see who could out kiss the other. They were both winning because they were conquerors. Their bodies moved together, tongues sliding and colliding in wicked-wild fashion, sucking hard.

The more her lips ravaged his, the more tension she could feel in his pants. Remembering vividly what was under that thin material wound her into a tight spring, ready to bounce free. The feel of his scrotum, the base of his thick rod, the heat from his juiced tip, his magnificent length—all of it lingered in the back of her mind. Fuck everything! She wanted him, right then and there.

Her hand moved to a strong, stiff cock, ready to rock. It pulled at the material, stretched it, made the zipper buckle, and she rubbed it with intense friction. Everything she'd tasted in her mouth over a week ago was back again, ready and steaming. The more she stroked him, the harder his kisses became, sucking her, nipping her own very hungry lips until he unwound her. His lips and erection did it for her, releasing pressure that was so intense that she could barely breathe. It soon flowed from her, releasing her, making her body faint, and her mind swim. Her lips quickly pulled away from his to ride out the rest of the wave. Her warm breath made contact with his already moist neck. Her voice quivered. "Jordan, my God, Jordan. What is it about you that makes me follow your trail?"

He pulled away from her. "I give you everything and what I just gave you, you needed. So did I. But if you need me so much, why do you make a conscious effort to avoid me?"

Reality check, brain freeze, culture shock! All of that in one, and she could barely respond. The ultimate point of her being there was to explain everything, her feelings, concerns. A kiss like that could systematically unbalance all checkbooks in the tristate area. She straightened in his arms, cleared her throat. "I'm here because I do need to explain my actions."

"I hope so, because you left my house without so much as a good-bye. I didn't know what I had done to deserve that. I still don't, Eve."

"Jordan, it's just that you're so different from me."

"Like black and white?"

"Like different lifestyles, Jordan. Color never mattered. I saw you and wanted you. Your touch was magic, your kisses were orgasms, your words so sweet . . . most of them."

"What do you mean?"

"We're so different, you and I. We lived totally different lives for so many years. I just don't know if the differences can mesh and, well, become one." She saw the confused look on his face. "Look, Jordan, I told you what my life was like— loving, full of family get-togethers, everything you didn't have. Your father did something. I don't know what, but it's something that'll be hard to work around. You don't believe in childhood. Remember when you said that?"

"Yeah. I didn't believe in mine because there wasn't one."

"What would that mean for us if we decided to take things further? I know I'm jumping the gun a little here, but I want kids, a good marriage, something my parents have. As far as I know, I want all of those things with you. But maybe you don't."

He leaned against one of the student desks, taking in a heavy sigh. "My life scares you, and I know this, Eve. I can't change who I am or what happened to me. All I can do is change my future." He took her hand again. "You're the only person who has made me want to change. I want all those things, too. I love children, I respect married couples, and hoped that by now I would be. It never worked for me, but I want it to. So far, from what I know about you, that could happen, but it'll take time. I can't change overnight."

She stroked his cheeks, wanting to kiss him again so badly and make him feel good again. But she had come to say something, make a stake in their reality, claim something. "I want you, Jordan. I want you more than any woman should be allowed to want a man. I believe in you for some reason, and I just want to know if we can work, if maybe we could take it a little slower, maybe even . . . date."

A sly smile crept across his face. "What about the kisses? Am I to be denied those wonderful kisses?"

"Not if you're willing to give me what I think I need, taking things slower. We started out with a bang, and our spaceship skyrocketed straight to the moon."

"You'll admit it was a fucking good ride, right?"

"It was, Jordan, and it can get better, if you want it to."

"I wanna be with you, Eve. I don't know what it is about you that made me move so quickly, but I'll do whatever you want, for however long it takes."

"Are you sure?"

He took her into his arms again. "Very sure. But for now, I need another kiss to get me through advanced Shakespeare with a bunch of snooty seniors. I have two classes back to back coming up."

"One kiss, then. And this kiss, Jordan, is going to be a killer!"

"Well, all right, girl!"

Three weeks later.

Jordan walked her to the door after an evening out on the town and kissed her passionately, not wanting to leave her but knew he had to. He withdrew from the succulent kiss and smiled into her cold face. "You get inside now. This wind is outrageous tonight."

"It is only February. And since it is so cold, why not come inside? Rest for a bit and let me make you some coffee before you drive to that big, cold mansion."

"Not tonight. I'm beginning to feel like a naughty boy all of a sudden. I've been good lately, coming inside, having a drink and some food and getting by with just kissing you. That's getting harder and harder, Eve. If I come in tonight, I really will *come in.* Know what I'm saying?"

She nipped at his lips again. "You have been a good boy, a

perfect boy, and it's been hard for me as well. Remember, I know what's in those pants, Jordan. I miss it, but ultimately it's better this way."

He shivered at the thought. "If you say so."

She slid her key into the lock. "Come on. You have to admit we've had fun together, and a bed hasn't even been in the picture. My family loves you."

"And I love them. I knew I would because only a certain type of family can have a wonderful daughter like you." His gloved hand smoothed across her face. "Maybe that's why I've really fallen for you."

His words made her forget the dangling key and the half-opened door. "Are you really falling for me?"

He pushed the door open. "Let's go inside. I don't want you freezing your tootsies off." Once inside the warm hallway of her home, he took her into his arms again, needing to taste her once more before braving a lonely drive back home. She would warm him for the ride, deliver good memories. For the first time in years, he actually had something that gave him good, lasting, potent memories. Sure, he had his share of potent remembrances, but none of them as loving as now. He gently pulled away from her, massaging her shivering shoulders. "I have an idea, if you're game for it."

"You've changed your mind about the coffee?"

"You know I can't stay here for that, Eve, because I'd never leave. But there is something I've wanted to discuss. I have winter break in two weeks. I'm meeting my brother at Indianhead Mountain Resort and was wondering if you'd like to join us. You know, spend quality time together."

"Skiing? I don't know a ski blade from a toothpick."

"You don't have to ski. There's lots of things up there for us to do, like ride the lifts with me and—" He moved in closer, "get stuck at the top of one and make out with me."

"That part of it sounds inviting, but we can do that here."

"This'll be fun for us. Have you ever been skiing?"

"Too busy with blackjack games on Friday nights."

"You're crazy, you know that? And, I'm crazy in love. I always rent a villa, the Phoenix. It has everything—cable television, a computer, fireplace, Jacuzzi, a kitchen so we can make hot chocolate." His brows wriggled. "Sound inviting?"

"Two weeks from now?"

"Think you can fit it in? I'll buy you some skiing outfits. You know, those tight-fitting spandex ski pants with huge Dale of Norway sweaters."

Her eyes lightened. "I do love those sweaters."

"Then have I lured you into joining me and my brother for a week full of fun-filled days, lots of excitement, and warm nights by a blazing fireplace?"

"With your brother there?"

"He always stays at the Roots Resort, so don't worry about him."

Eve snuggled into his warm coat, feeling where the melted flakes puddled against it. She kissed his full lips ever so lightly, teasing him, wishing the fireplace wasn't so far away. It would be nice to get away for a week, max out, see how the other half lives. "I'd love to go. Where exactly is Indianhead?"

"Wakefield, Michigan."

"Wakefield! Do you know how far into the upper peninsula that is?"

"The best snow is there; so are the warmest resorts and cabins. C'mon, give it a try. Don't you want to be with me?"

More and more each day. "Okay, Dale of Norway, you've got me. Just don't expect me to do any damn yodeling from some mountain and scamper around in flowery shorts with suspenders."

"Only if they're Daisy Dukes."

"Like you'd know about those."

"I know more than you think. What I know at this very moment is that if I don't get out of here, I'll break every promise I made to you."

"Not just yet." She stroked his warm cheeks. "I'd still like to take it kind of slow, even up there. Can you do that?"

"So long as the prize is still mine."

"I'm yours, Jordan. I just need to make sure it stays that way."

"You got it, baby. Lock this door behind me. Can't have anyone taking my girl from me." His lips tugged at hers once again, slowly, softly, seductively; then he pulled away. "I'll call you in a few days."

"Call me when you get home." She watched him go to his snow-dusted car, then closed the door, and leaned against it. She was falling hard for a man she had only known a little over a month. It took every ounce of her inner fiber not to go back on her word and take him into her bedroom. Night after night of watching movies with him, making him romantic dinners, just talking with smooth jazz on the CD player was becoming increasingly hard, but she did it and felt good about it. Tempting him was the key, though. It would show her more of the man she knew he was.

Eve's eyes beamed at the sight of the winter hideaway and the tall trees surrounding it. It was so big. Getting used to his mansion was one thing, but this was something else. Her eyes widened as they walked with their suitcases up the freshly snowplowed walkway. "What room are we in, Jordan?"

"Room? What do you mean room? The place is ours, at least for a week."

"You're kidding. The entire place?"

"I told you I rented a villa. Though I'd be glad to share a gunnysack as long as we were together."

She took his hand and proceeded up the long walkway. "Having dinner with Joseph was a blast. He's so funny, and you two look so much alike. Then again, you always have."

"How do you know that?"

"I woke up on our first night together, after you rocked my body till kingdom come and fell asleep. There was a photo album on the coffee table in the den. I looked through and saw the cutest little boys, but one had tears in his eyes."

"There's still tears, but of a different kind."

"Happy ones?"

"Never happier." He slid the key into the lock and pushed the door open. "I have you to thank for that, Ms. Harlan."

Maybe one day that Ms. will change to Mrs. She could only hope she was being steered in the right direction down lover's lane. He was coming along nicely, wanting to live another kind of life, one filled with card games on Friday nights and chicken frying in the pan. He was learning to be a homey; it looked good on him, and Eve liked it.

Of all the winter sports on the agenda, Eve liked the cross-country skiing best, even though she fell five times during a brief one-mile run. What was most romantic was getting caught on the bunny lift in the dead of night and making out over the highest hill. It scared her at first, but Jordan was so warm and reassuring, and the minute his moist lips met hers, all fear vanished. What took its place was a stimulating feeling between her thighs. Only Jordan could supply that, and she made the best of it by riding the twisting, turning wave of an orgasm right there on that tight ski lift. The stars were their only guiding lights.

Her first two evenings had been so jam-packed and fun-filled that she couldn't help but wonder what he had planned after watching him and his brother race down the main slope. He had told her that after he tried beating his brother on the slopes, the evening would be theirs.

She could hardly wait. His surprises were always so . . . *enticing.*

After getting her fill of a fabulous dinner that Jordan made for her, which consisted of homemade lobster bisque laced with sherry, Lake Michigan trout, garden salad, and baby potatoes, she snuggled near the big picture window of the villa. The evening sky looked chilly yet inviting as the snow continued to cover the treetops and mountain ranges. The feeling her amaretto-spiked hot chocolate was giving her certainly hadn't hampered the romantic mood. She could hear Jordan in the kitchen splashing around, busting suds, insistent on her not doing a damn thing that night other than relaxing and hopefully being his faithful concubine later that evening.

It was time, and Eve knew it. Jordan had been a good boy, making strides and being ever so patient with her. The truth of the matter was, Eve was the one with that growing yearning welling deep within her core. Kissing Jordan and giving him palm rubs and back massages was a true enough thrill, but she needed the action, craved it each night he left her.

Jordan crept in behind her, but she could smell his approach. He had a naturalness to him, earthy yet manly enough to intoxicate her to sexual peaks. She let him play his game of sneak attacks, felt his hands massaging her shoulders, loosening her tight muscles and working his way down her heavy ski sweater. "This material is much too thick, Eve. I can hardly feel you."

"You said you like it on me, that the colors match my skin tone."

"The only real thing that matches your skin tone is me, though I am a little pale."

"You're not pale. Actually, you have a goldenness about you, and those green eyes makes me want you even more."

"I've got something else that can make you want me more." He slipped into the lounger next to her, toting his own spirited chocolate, and nestled against her sweater. They both stared through the window, watching the snow continue to blanket the world. Jordan broke their moments of stillness. "Have the past few days been everything you thought they would be?"

"They have. I've always wanted to go to a ski resort but never really had the opportunity." A smile crept across her rosy brown cheeks. "Actually, I've always wanted to lounge around a ski resort and drink my fill of hot chocolate and pig out on delicious food. That's really the extent of my snow-bunny sports."

"You look so good doing just that. You and tight ski pants were meant to be together. Besides, they work better than bulky pants."

"Better for what?"

"The slopes you're getting on in the morning."

"No way, Jordan! Black people and ski slopes aren't a good match. Though I must say you looked good today losing to your brother."

"He always wins against me in everything. I don't care because he and I have so much fun together."

She moved into him, sliding her hand into his sweater. His muscles tightened to the caress of her hand. His reaction sent warm chills across her skin. God, how she missed feeling him pounding away inside her, sliding against her moisture, stretching her juiced sex with rugged thrusts. He was so good at delivering awesome friction against a vibrating clit. He was the only man who could do it right . . . *do her right.* She missed that, missed him, and now, stroking his chest was really putting a hurting on her self-restraint. They'd both come so close on many occasions but had held off. Eve felt she could no longer hold off, not with him in her arms, stroking his nipples, lifting his sweater, savoring the exotic taste of his skin with her hungry tongue. She moaned against the feathery-light hair trailing his navel. "Your brother hasn't won everything, Jordan."

He released a deep breath and relaxed against the chaise lounger. "Really? What have I won?"

"A woman who's now ready to give into you, to be your slave, your anything." Her hand slid to his bulging member pressing so hard against spandex pants. She worked it up and down gently, soon replacing her hand with her lips, sucking his tip through the material as she fingered his tight sac. There was so much power there, so much strength, and she needed to experience it again. She was ready for him, needed to feel a lover satisfying every orifice of her body, poking into every hole he could find and saturating her with his cream.

Eve knew nothing would matter until she commenced with him up there in that snow-covered, secluded hideaway. Everything would again make sense once her body got what it needed. Her lips parted from the dampened material, and she stared up at him. His head was resting against the slope of the seat, as she stared up into the high ceiling, mesmerized by what she was doing to him. "Jordan. I want to."

His eyes met hers, his voice strained, as he gathered rational thought after almost coming. "Are you sure, Eve? I want this to be right for you."

"It is right for me. Making love to you is always right for me. I have this overpowering need to taste you, Jordan—taste you in ways that I've missed so much by being stupid."

"You weren't being stupid, just in need of some reassurance. I did move fast with you, but only because you were—are—a gem that I couldn't afford to let slip away." He stroked her cheeks, fingered her trembling lips, then spread his legs on either side of the lounger. "Take it, Eve."

She was like a child at Christmas, and what a large, lovely package she had to unwrap. He was already busting at the seams from want of her, and that's what triggered her chain reaction. She sucked that hardened, clothed tip again to build friction, feeling his penis rise under the fabric. As she went deeper onto him, pulling at the material, she felt his veins, his sac tightening, his hips pressing feverishly against her as they begged for release, freedom.

Eve tugged at his pants, pulling them down and seeing his seething erection bounce into her life. He was so stiff and hard, as if he had been saving all that perfect cream for weeks, just for her—all for her.

Her small hand gripped him, barely able to wrap around such an erection. She massaged him before letting her tongue snake out and devour him. The minute her tongue met the slit of his engorged tip, she became ravenous. Her lips surrounded him, pulled on him. She could barely get enough as she massaged his scrotum and gently squeezed. She could feel his life force within his sac and needed him to pump it into her.

Jordan moaned, liking it, loving it, wanting more and more of it. His hips slid up and down the leather lounger, ducking his length so deep within her warm mouth that he could barely think straight. He pulled at his sweater until it lifted over his head, revealing more to her. The thought of being in clothing around her seemed too stupid for thought.

The same for her. She pulled free from his phallus, staring at the engorged tip as she slipped from her own sweater. Her eyes never left him, and once the garment was off, she went back to work on him, rubbing her tongue against the underside of his cock and feathering her way down to his base.

Jordan unsnapped her bra, taking her breasts into his palms and working them. Her erect nipples tickled his fingers, making him harder the more he gently squeezed them. One hand moved to her back, stroking up and down before moving into her spandex pants to stroke her behind. Jordan moved in tighter, needing to feel her dampened sex, press into it, let her moisture cover his flesh like a second skin.

He made contact with her derriere, fingering down to her soaking core, and slid the wetness between her cheeks. Her magic with his penis drove him to madness, needing to strip her of everything and feed that giant rod into her tight, slippery opening. Until she had her fill, he teased her in other ways. Two fingers slid into her, pushing and pulling, stimulating a clit that was ready for combustion. It quivered against his fingers, and she pulled away from him long enough to ride out a shattering orgasm. She called to him, bucked against him, pleaded into his flushed face. His only words: "It's coming, baby."

He stood with that bobbing cock stretched out to the world and stepped from his pants and shoes. Removing everything from Eve was next. He pulled her anxious body to his, kissed her long and hard, letting her feel the pressure from his erection shifting against her. His kisses moved down her neck and onto her breasts, licking them, nibbling on taut nipples as he slid her pants down her legs.

Eve gladly stepped from them, then pointed to the lounger. Her voice giddy, her body tingling. "Lay back down, Jordan, and let me mount you."

With his bare backside against the buttery soft leather, he looked up and anxiously awaited her descent. He braced her arms on either side of his head and helped her to get parallel with him. Once she was in the perfect spot for absolute penetration, he let her do her thing.

Eve kissed his hungry lips again until all that pent-up frustration was ready to bubble from her. She lifted her derriere higher, positioning herself over him, then slid down, feeling his tip poke her opening. She teased by lifting back up, then down again, repeating the sequence until they both were lost in desire. Eve lowered again, guiding him slowly into her, adjusting to his size, letting him enter her until she constricted in waves around him. Her jaw trembled from pure ecstasy as he plummeted deeper into her, rocking her, gyrating around her clit as if it were on a mission. *It was.*

Jordan jerked around inside of her, and he massaged her breasts, making them bump and jump against his hands as his strokes increased. He made her ride him high and dry, working his body, sweating, panting. Both twisted and turned against each other so much that they slid to the carpet.

Jordan landed on top, and one look down at Eve made him thrust hard, drilling her until they moved across the room. She yielded to him, yet stayed so strong, and that's what he loved about her—so sexy, so faceted, so everything to him. As he moved mercilessly against her, he couldn't help but smile. There she was tonight, bare to him, yet so clad with everything a woman was born to have—heat, sweet nectar, rawness, and love. That alone made him pump harder until he gave, spilling so much liquid into her that it was seeping from her.

Eve rode his volcano until she erupted, clinching him, jerking what was not hidden of his maleness against her hands. His scrotum was so warm in her hands as she palmed it. At the precise moment, everything magnified, became clear, loud and amazing. She screamed his name until that spiraling sensation within her frame arrested, leaving her diminished but loving the feeling.

Jordan landed on top of her, out of breath and out of his mind. Life itself wasn't as delicious as she had just been to him. Was she real? Or a figment of his overactive imagination? Then he felt her damp hair and skin. Certainly real.

He kissed her wet face, lifted her into his arms, and carried her to a bedroom that housed a lit fireplace.

Again, Eve awakened in the wee hours of the morning, but the only difference was that this time there was a hot, stiff erection between her thighs. She let it stay there, playing at her opening along with his large fingers. Two of them slipped into her sex, manipulated her still swollen labia. Within moments, she felt Jordan slide down, hold one of her legs up, and bury his face in her core. His tongue and fingers accosted her in vigorous strokes. The fingers subsided only to make way for more tongue that lapped at her, stroking her from stem to stern, swirling around and tickling flesh. When she came, she could feel Jordan's teeth nipping at the quivering clit and tasting her like he'd never had anything that scrumptious before. The sounds he made while devouring her made her come again. His groans, utterances, lapping sounds, all of it combined to send shock waves through her body.

With her back now resting against the mattress, she was free to spread-eagle for him from east to west. The wider her legs parted for his insatiable lust, the wilder he became. She could feel an orgasm slowly welling inside, picking up pace like a tornado, twisting, turning, and yearning to spin out of control. Senses heightened to fever pitch, nervous hands grabbed her breasts, feeling the tight points, but that was all she could do to stop from ravaging him in the process. She was ready—real ready.

Jordan's arms tightened around her thighs, pulling her closer to the edge of the bed. He continued tickling her fancy, sucking it, blowing on it, spreading her pubic hair aside to get to more of her flesh. There was no way in hell any woman could feel and taste the way she did. Maybe she wasn't real, just a figment of his starving imagination, and that "imagination" made him bury his face deeper and deeper into honey. When she came, her lips quivered against his, pounding a super-hot clitoris against his hungry tongue. Her cries educated him to what real desire and passion was. He knew it well now, so well that he stood to his feet, hoisted her hips to match his, and shoved his untamed rod wildly into her. He bucked, jerked, stiffened, and continued to jam. Throaty words escaped him in volumes. "Let me do you, baby, all night. Scream for me, girl. Tell me you love this seething pipe tearing you to shreds."

That was it! Even his words drove her to sexual insanity. Tears rolled down her cheeks as she called to him. Her hands scratched at his, needing to touch him, feel his sensitive skin against hers. Her sixth orgasm of the evening shattered her, ransacked her body, and did the same to him. His nectar saturated her hands and breasts as he pulled out and delivered.

The last drop dripped down the side of his phallus, and he lay his drenched body across hers.

Eve could still feel her sex quaking in spasms, yet she felt so hollow from his missing length. She faced him, smiled as she caressed his warm, wet lips. "Was it that good, Jordan? Good enough to take your breath away?"

"Yeah . . . oh, yeah. That was sensational, awe-inspiring lovemaking."

She moved closer into him, feeling his still hard erection against her stomach. "You are the most incredible man I've ever known. Sex with you is . . ."

"Unbelievable," he finished for her.

"I take it you're enjoying our vacation?"

"Very much."

"I'm planning a big future with you, Eve, if you still want one with me. I'll give you everything you've always wanted. *Everything*."

Eve fell asleep in Jordan's arms that night. Love. Trust. Super sex. She had it all at last. She'd met her match finally, someone who would never want another woman. There was no other woman for him and no other man for her.

shopping. shoes. sex.

1

---

the pretty-man syndrome

Every now and then, all women are hit hard by the pretty-man syndrome, and Amber Donohue was no exception. She thought she'd had a case of pretty-man syndrome with Maurice some years ago but never quite succumbed. He was in love with himself, and after six months of doing everything he wanted to do, Amber was tired of it. Eventually she left him alone to have that single-minded love affair, and from what she last heard, he was still hovering somewhere over Lake Michigan with an engagement ring *she* had purchased. Amber moved on, but the syndrome struck her again, and hard.

For those unaware, the pretty-man syndrome is simply this: One day a man struts past you who's so pretty and sexy that you can't stand the sight of any other man. Upon contact with Jason DeMaras, Amber was caught in that infamous web; thus, this is the story of how Amber got her groove on.

The setting: Somerset Mall in Troy, Michigan—a place where those with money have a blast. For everyone else, window-shopping was the sport of the day. Amber didn't give a damn about that. She may not have had the most money in the world, but she was fly as hell and dressed as though she were more than a mere jewelry shop owner. She had just gotten her hair done at Glamour Glitz; Jackie could certainly hook a girl up, and for the right price. Amber laid out the greenbacks and exited looking like the queen she was—hair in a short bob, longer on the neck and sides, make-up laid, making her pretty, fair complexion glow. The girl was boss with a capital B as she walked through Saks Fifth Avenue wearing tight black jeans, a crystal earring-necklace set, and a flowery pink and black top with a neckline so deep that a man's toes would curl if he laid eyes on her.

She was heading through Somerset Mall because that was where all the juicy men were. Her mission at first was a pair of Ferragamo pumps, no shorter than three inches. They'd look cool for her sister's wedding in July, but it was only May, and she planned on looking on jam way before that, and just for the heck of looking sexy to the men in the mall. Yes, she'd wear the pumps out of the store. Her second mission; looking at cute salesmen. Knowing Somerset, there would be a slew of them at her beck and damn call.

Neiman Marcus had their share of fine salesmen, but the shoes weren't hot enough, being either too small, too large, or in the wrong color. Moving on! Gucci had the opposite—gorgeous shoes, yet out of her price range and salesmen who were nothing to write home about. Again, moving on.

There was a quaint little shoe boutique, Roma Shoes, on the other side of the mall near the MAC counter, a place she had to stop at, anyway. Why not make two trips in one, was her thinking. That boutique got her attention months back for two reasons. They had all the famous makers, like Sesto Meucci, Vaneli, everything Italian; but the main reason was that she saw something in there that almost blew her mind. It was a day she had to leave the house because nothing was going right, and she had to clear her mind. She entered Roma, not looking or feeling her best, but shoes always brought out the best in her. While window-shopping, a man whizzed by her who took her breath away. She couldn't see his full face, but his profile was to kill for. He never faced her, but she exited the store staring at him. She left without shoes or the pretty man, but she never forgot him.

Six months later, Amber strolled back in there with her hair looking too together for even her own benefit and felt warning signs of the pretty-man syndrome again. She tried staying away from it because she knew she'd been hit hard just by looking at this fellow. Before she could get past the entrance, she saw him from the corner of her eye and knew who he was—that pretty-profile man from months back. She was really too nervous to look him straight in the face but knew it was the same man. She could feel it in her bones, let alone see it with her eyes: beautiful golden-bronze skin, big dark eyes, and a sexy little moustache just aching for a woman to run her tongue across it. If that wasn't all that and a bag of chips, too, he was tall and sporting a beautiful physique. He was just looking too good in his butter yellow dress shirt, cinnamon brown slacks, and matching tie. Juicy!!

Amber pretended to be looking for a pair of heels, but her mind couldn't concentrate on shoes after catching his scent. The only thing running through her mind was, *Oh my God. I can't believe he's actually facing me, after wondering so long how handsome he was.* Her own thoughts were making her nervous, sweaty, not knowing how she was going to react once coming face-to-face with him. She hadn't expected him to be quite that beautiful. Slowly, she turned around to see if someone could look that good in real life.

He'd been talking to his coworker and Amber had gotten a hint of their conversation. The two men had been discussing her leather-clad feet—a pair of red and white Pumas. She'd forgotten the heels that day, despite how she loved looking fly. Once her eyes met with the trueness of his sensuality, she was floored, though she played it off well, smiling in his direction.

She had heard part of the conversation about her shoes and knew that being the salesman he was, he would approach. However, she didn't think that that was his sole mission, knowing she looked good, and that thought alone made her swoon. Hardly any fine men approached her. She was used to the usual

Pleistocene men and men from the Cretaceous era and your regular Pygmies. No one other than Maurice had ever taken much interest in little ole shy Amber, who was losing that shyness by the microsecond all of the sudden.

Amber soon realized the pretty thing did not need glasses, as he was on his way over to make her acquaintance. He cleared his voice. "We were just discussing your shoes. What are they?"

Though she was a nervous wreck around pretty men, no matter how confident she was in other parts of her life, she managed a sane response. "Oh, these are just Pumas. I got my black and white ones in Manhattan last summer while attending a conference."

He moved in closer. "Sounds like you're a busy young woman, and busy women need great shoes to keep them going."

"That's why I'm here. I tried the other stores, but they didn't have anything that piqued my interest." Taking one look at him definitely did the trick. She'd have been too glad to spend the night there in his arms, screw the shoes.

"You went to other stores before coming to mine? That was your first mistake."

"And my second one?"

"Not hanging around on your first visit long enough to let me put my boxes down."

That took her. No way in hell did she even imagine him seeing her all those months ago, let alone remember her. "You saw me a few months back?"

"Yes, ma'am, and what a sight you were. Too bad you didn't stay around to give me a real thrill."

"I was at my worst, yet you remembered me?"

"A beautiful woman is hard to forget. Besides, I saw how your earrings sparkled. What are they, crystals?"

"You know your stones, don't you?"

His eyes barely scanned her frame. "That and other things. Where'd you get them from?"

"I made them."

"No way! Wow, you really are a busy girl. They're absolutely beautiful, like their creator."

Amber ate that up, beaming at him. "Really, you're too kind."

He briefly scouted the room before moving in closer to her. "Kind? That would be someone other than me, but I'm serious—you're absolutely beautiful, and so is your jewelry. Looks like what we sell in here, only better, more exotic. Do you sell any?"

The minute he moved in closer, she could smell his aftershave, and it smelled like erotic sex; with him, it mixed well. Too well. Suddenly she found herself fighting for self-control. "I own my own jewelry shop on Main. It's not opened yet. I'm getting the financing together." Amber knew only one thing: If she didn't get the hell away from him, she'd spill the beans and let him know exactly how she felt about him. That had always been her problem with cute men, telling them too prematurely how sexy they were. At that, she walked across the room to a pair of red croc pumps, hoping he wouldn't follow. Wrong, he followed as though she were Little Bo Peep. She didn't lose any sheep but was about to gain a wolf.

He followed close behind her. "So, what's the name of your shop?"

Surprised that a man was that infatuated with her, she met him face-to-face. "You're really interested?"

"Sure. Come on, let me in on it."

"I named it Exotica Jewels."

"Good name; fits the owner to a T, if you don't mind me saying."

With the red pump still in her hand, she faced him and held it up, speechless. He beat her to the punch. "Would you like to see that in your size?"

"I, uh . . ." He left her speechless, breathless. She didn't know what to do with all that nervous energy he suddenly gave her. He was beautiful; so different from Maurice because he actually had a personality. He was everything she craved. Then that infectious Amber Donohue smile crossed her lovely face. "Actually, if you don't mind me saying"—her voice raised from pure excitement—"you are so damn handsome." The words she feared she'd say one way or another if he didn't leave her alone, which he wasn't planning on. Well, it was said and done, and she hoped she could live with the consequences.

"Me, handsome? Thanks. I hardly hear that from a beautiful woman, let alone one with so much going for her; one that's probably too busy making jewelry to buy shoes."

"No, when a woman needs shoes, she really means it. I am busy enough." The pump still dangled from her hand as she continued speaking. "The funny thing is, I've got a BS degree in education with a minor in marketing from Howard, yet I sit around making jewelry and writing erotica romance." Oops! She didn't want that out, either. Maybe she did. She figured the better the bait, the more you could reel in the really big mackerel—but this one was a tiger shark.

"Erotica romance? My goodness, what is it that you don't do?"

"There's plenty, trust me."

"I'd love to read that erotica. What is your name, anyway? Sorry, but I forgot to ask; you know, too busy scoping the merchandise—yours. You'll have to forgive me. I don't get many beautiful women in here. The women who come in have high hopes that a pair of heels can turn a prizefighter into a queen. How wrong they are."

"And you still don't have that beauty in your store." She extended her hand. "I'm Amber Donohue."

She took his hand, and from his mere touch, she knew he was something to reckon with. His eyes were so dark and mysterious, lips so kissable, and that perfect caramel-brown complexion was so ready to be tasted. She was caught. Nothing else existed, not the store, other workers, nothing. Sex oozed from him, and all she wanted was to have some of it—his.

His voice brought her back to the real world. "I'm Jason

DeMaras." He was reluctant to let go of her hand simply to grab his business card from the front desk. He'd touched the hand of an erotic queen, and there was no going back. The pit he had fallen in was too deep to crawl from. He did manage not to stumble over his words. "Take my card and call me anytime. I'm always here. I'd love to exhibit your jewelry. I think you'd sell a ton; that'd be good for you and the store."

"Would that be *good* for you? What I mean is, would you get a commission?"

"I know exactly what you mean, and, yes, it would definitely be good for me."

His seductive smile knocked her into next month. She looked at his business card and fingered the raised printing, wishing it was his chest she was intricately caressing, but for the time being, the card had to do. No doubt he'd pushed her over the edge and landed her smack in the middle of the infamous pretty-man syndrome—a heck of a place to be. Then reality hit again, and her only thought, *please don't be another Maurice.*

"Sure I can't interest you in a pair of shoes? I have a pair that I'd love to slide you into. My man Kenneth Cole has a nice, supple pair of Italian leather pumps perfect for a working woman; the perfect shoe to enhance the beauty of a true treasure."

Her mind was swimming, her body vibrating with the thought of what he could slide deeply into her. Unfortunately, Roma shoes were a little too expensive for her that day, although she knew how good she'd look in them.

"My intent was to buy shoes today, but the prices are a little steep for me in this mall. I should have known that. Maybe you can hold a pair for me, you know, select something nice and cute, then give me a week to come in for them."

"Like I said, I have the perfect pair. All you have to do is say yes, and they're yours, Ms. Donohue. Tell you what, I will put them aside. When you come in, try them on. If they're not for you, I do have something else."

Indeed you do, Mr. Fine as Hell Jason DeMaras.

"You must do me one favor. Bring in a few of your pieces, let me send them to headquarters."

"You'd really do that for me?"

He scanned her once again. "From what I see, the designs are on jam. Oh yeah, so is your jewelry."

That statement, coupled with his sensual smile, almost depleted her to a puddle in the middle of the floor. "That's a promise. You're some guy, Mr. DeMaras."

"That I am. One more thing—I'd love to read your erotica. If it reads as good as you look. Damn!"

"Thank you, and I'd love for you to read some. It is a little on the hot side."

"I'm counting on it."

My God . . . too hot to trot. This man wants to read my secret thoughts, my explicit secret thoughts. Should I really let him? After all, he is a stranger. Give 'em up, girl, and let pretty-boy Jason into your wildest dreams. The battle of the id and ego was on! "I have a few that are on jam. When I can get some pictures together with the jewelry, I'll bring them in along with the stories. Will that do?"

"Depends on how long we're talking."

"When would you like them?"

Again, he moved so close to her that she could smell his chromosomes. He took her hand into his, feeling her smooth skin, toying with her delicate wrists. "As soon as possible."

"You are a glutton for punishment."

His voice lowered. "And I need to be spanked for being so bad."

He released her hand and gave her a nice, juicy hug. She could feel every muscle in his body pressing against her. He felt so good and warm as her hands glided down to the small of his back, stayed there, smoothing his undershirt against his slightly moist skin. When they parted, she looked into his eyes. He'd been blushing. She was so glad to be the reason for a pretty man to blush.

After leaving, she felt giddy, like a schoolgirl with her first crush, and she stayed on cloud nine the entire day. She didn't know how she managed to drive the Honda home without crashing it into a stone wall somewhere on Woodward Avenue. From that day on, she ate, drank, and slept Jason. Jason this, Jason that. Her mind was obsessed with him. Since then, she replayed that day in her mind over and over again and couldn't wait until she saw him again. Amber meant to get him any way she could, even if she had to spend every waking moment making jewelry to sell in his store. That was all right with her since that's what she did for a living, anyway.

Amber stayed on that proverbial cloud even through work, the classes she was taking, everything. Each night before her eyes closed, she would reach over to the nightstand and pick up his card. She was mesmerized by the way his name looked, and she fingered the letters much the way a woman touches her man while they make love. That was what Amber wanted, to make love to him, seduce him, stroke him, taste him, make him think of no woman but her. She didn't care about anything else. He was the one—Jason, Jason, Jason. She had to have him.

Later that evening . . .

Amber got to work on the contract for her new store on Main, right down the street from Somerset Mall. And while she was waiting for it to go through, she thought about how great it would be to work down the street from him, have lunch with him every day, and hopefully dinner every night. Amber was never one to press issues or to force herself on someone, but she could think of nothing but jewelry and Jason, the double Js. When something got in her head, she either had to take care of it or let it drive her insane. She chose the first. The store contract was looking good, but Jason was looking better. She put everything in motion and was ready to make a move.

2

making moves

A month later, Amber still hadn't gotten her digital camera fixed. It decided to break in the middle of a picture-taking session of her malachite pieces. But that hadn't stopped her. It had been a month since coming down with pretty-man syndrome, and she knew she had to get in there to see Jason soon. There was no cure for what she had, other than to look into his eyes and pretend she was going into his back room to find shoes. Yeah, she wanted to find shoes all right, and make him slip something right into her—his own personal shoehorn, well oiled and glistening. That was the very word—*into*—into the sweetness, into the pleasure.

Two weeks later, she entered the mall with her mom and sister Geneva and peeked around the corridor to see if he was in his store, not sure if he even worked on Sundays. There was another man standing in the store, the same one who had been there before. He'd been good enough to let Jason have at her, but where was her Jason now?

She smiled and waved at him, knowing he remembered her, as every man seemed to do nowadays, though she still didn't know why. Much to her surprise, Jason looked around to see what his coworker was waving at and he spotted her. He smiled and waved, too, making Amber's day. He motioned for her to come over, but Amber decided to take care of the other mall stuff, giving herself more time to spend in the lap of luxury.

By twelve, she was aching for a good dose of Jason DeMaras's hands somewhere on her body. Ditching her mom and sister was normally the last thing she would ever do, but Jason could not be compromised, not in her book. What she had to tell them eventually was an utter lie, but it worked nonetheless—she had to look for a dress for an upcoming shower. Since her mom and sister were both out there for kitchen utensils, looking for a dress was the last thing they wanted to do.

All three booked in different directions, and Amber was free—free to enter Roma Shoes and dream her little dream. Why not? She'd been a fool for a man before, why not for one with sense, a job, and a body to slaughter for? She wanted him to own her—mind, body and soul.

When she turned the corner, there he was, standing in the front of the store looking bored, but that was about to change. Remembering the content of the short story she gave him weeks before, she knew that the moment their eyes met, the excitement would start.

One look at beautiful Mr. Jason set her mind ablaze. He was sporting a maroon silk dress shirt and black slacks. They looked so good against his brown complexion that she almost lost it right there in that crowded mall. No matter what her panties were doing, her feet were making tracks toward him; and for some reason, the closer she got, the more nervous she became. Amber Donohue was really just a skittish teenager in a thirty-two-year-old body, a bunch of bundled-up nerves, but they were the good kind of nerves, making her tingle all over from the good stuff life had to offer. Her feet moved faster.

Jason saw her approaching and extended his arms, all too happy that the queen of the mall was within his reach again. And Amber did exactly what he wanted her to do—move swiftly into his body, making him hard again in all the right places, keeping his heart so warm for a stranger who was suddenly not so strange. His voice broke with heightened anticipation. "Amber. Where you been, girl?"

Once their bodies parted, they stared hungrily at each other, as though the good thing would leave if they weren't careful to trap it. Amber lingered on his honey-coated smile as her body ached for just one more touch. She'd spent too much time eating, drinking and sleeping Jason DeMaras. Nothing existed in her mind but the very idea of him; and how his naked, slick body would feel next to hers; yet, she had to force her lips to move, to do something else other than tremble from want of a juicy kiss.

As like him, her voice communicated excitement that was too hard to mask. "I've been, well, working. I finally got the land contract for my store. That alone was work beyond work."

He took her hands into his. "That's great! I remember you saying something about squaring things away. Now I have a place to visit my favorite customer."

"How can I be your favorite customer when I haven't bought one pair of shoes from you?"

"I'll say it like this: there's more to life than securing a purchase." He moved in closer. "Besides, when you're in the store, I do my own bit of shopping. Get what I'm saying?"

She beamed. "You really are too kind, Jason."

He quickly looked around at the small crowd beginning to enter the mall. "Come on in. It's just Malcolm and myself in the store until two-thirty, and he's busy with inventory. Plenty of time to chat. That and look at stunning shoes that belong on pretty feet. I held a pair aside for you."

"You did? Cool! The red pair, right?"

"You got it, but I've really got to talk to you about that story, girl."

"You liked it?"

"In two words, hell yeah!"

They sat side by side on the back loveseat, so close to each other that Amber could feel his thigh on hers, feeling heat pulsating from him, hot lava from a hot male. Again, his eyes met hers with such excitement and heat, and a smile that melted her down.

"Girl, that story! It was, well, it did things to portions of my body that shall remain nameless for now."

"Then my plan worked all too well. However, I expected to see you when I dropped it off the other day. They said you were off, and I made them promise me you'd get it."

I'd love to get it, he thought. "They made sure it was in my hands the minute I stepped into the store. I read it at home that night, in the privacy of my own bedroom."

"What a bedroom that must be."

He moved a bit closer. "It could be, but it's lonely."

"I don't believe that. Someone as hot as you are should have women crawling all over you."

"Thanks, but I'm picky, waiting for the right woman. Speaking of such, you don't look like someone who would write erotica."

"Really? How should someone look who writes them?"

"What I'm saying is, you look like the kind of woman those stories are written about."

"No way! My heroines are always exotic. They live exotic lives, engage in exotic sex, have exotic men at their beck and call. Believe me, that's not me."

"I beg to differ. I loved the story; hotter than I anticipated." He leaned back and looked at her, sporting a sly smile. "All that hot, seething sex coming from one hot, seething woman—none other than Ms. Amber Marie Donohue. I wanted to be in that story so bad that I was sweating."

"Glad I could do that to you." Her brows furrowed, re-membering his last sentence. "How do you know my name is Amber Marie Donohue? I never told you my middle—"

"Another customer came in wearing exotic wire-wrapped crystals the other day, and I asked about them. She gave your name. Believe me, I'm not psychic enough to know anything like that. The only thing I know are gut feelings."

"And let me guess, your gut feeling is telling you I need a pair of Enzos."

"I don't think you'd like to know what my true feelings are. I did hold a nice pair that would be perfect for you, but I want you to give me something first."

Mind on overdrive and leaving earth immediately. The sensually handsome Jason DeMaras needed something from her, a merely attractive woman. Suddenly, wanting to know a man's gut feeling was top priority; something that ceased to exist along with her ex, Maurice. He never cared about anything other than how he looked to himself in the mirror.

Amber thought her voice was beyond quivering, but as usual, she came out smelling like a rose, and sounding like a queen. Soon, she hoped, one with a new king. "What would I possibly have that you would want?"

"I shouldn't answer that, but I will. Another story."

Her deflated heart made her weak. Naturally, her mind went on a whirlwind adventure, thinking about him whisking her into his arms, taking her into the back room, and doing all those delicious, dirty things that she'd written about and was brazen enough to give to him. Nope, his fancy centered around another story instead of getting the real thing firsthand. Reality awakened her. "If you let me try on the Enzos, I'll bring in another story next week. Deal?"

"Be right back." He looked down at her feet. "Eight and a half, right?"

"You know it all, don't you?"

"Only with customers I concentrate on."

Within minutes, he was back, as though being separated from her one more minute would kill him. Yes, her hot little story had bitten him hard, turned him into a testosterone-pumping mass of hard muscles, and the boner he was beginning to sport was indicative of his feelings. He eagerly plopped the boxes down and went to work on someone he'd wanted to touch intimately going on a month now. His voice deepened as he spoke. "I have a pair of red three-inch pumps;

leather so buttery smooth that they'll make you feel like you're walking on air. Let's try them."

Hell of a salesman? He certainly was. The sound of his voice buttering up those buttery leather pumps sold her, and feeling them, along with his fingers on the underside of her foot, really took her there. A raspy, "Slide them on," got them both going.

Jason quickly removed the first shoe from the box, slowly pulling the balled paper from it, stretching it, lengthening it, then finally jerking it out. Amber watched his antics, knowing exactly what the fuck he was doing, and she liked it—a lot. She wanted to pull and stretch him much the same way.

Next, he slid the footy on. The feel of his smooth, incredibly long fingers soothing and stroking her bare foot made her almost slide from the chair. Composure was a hell of a thing to hold on to at that time, but she tried her best, not wanting him to know that she would gladly lie down in the middle of the store with him, pull her panties off in front of everyone, and let him slid in easily, quickly, and pound away mercilessly inside of her. In the past, her thoughts were known to get her in trouble, but if she didn't stop thinking about what Jason could do to her, they'd both get arrested. So what? It would be worth a little jail time just to see him slide his zipper down.

Jason slid the pump on slowly, smoothly, evenly, then secured it by trapping it in his hand for a better fit. "Does that feel good?"

Mesmerized, Amber forgot she was on earth. The tightness of her groin twisted her into knots. The throbbing between her thighs from just looking at him was almost too much to bear, and all she could say was a weak, "Yes, it feels wonderful."

"May we try the other? I wouldn't want you walking around in that new shop of yours in pain."

"No, we wouldn't want that, would we?"

"No. Nothing but the best for Ms. Amber Marie. By the way, when do I get to see this new shop of yours?"

"Any time Jason wants to. I . . . uh, mean, when do you want to come in?"

"Now would be the perfect time to *slide* inside." Their eyes met, lingered on what they wanted so much—each other. "What I mean is, I'd love to come by but my hours here are so long and tight."

Long and tight, just what she wanted. "Really? How late do you work?"

"We close at ten, usually; eight tomorrow night. I tidy up things before I leave. Would that be too late?"

"It's my shop now. I can keep it open as long as I want to. Usually by ten I'm in my little bed, ready to watch *Golden Girls*, but for you, I'll stay open." *Wide open.*

A tantalizing smile crossed his face. "You'll stay open for me?"

"Anytime."

"I'll take that into consideration, pretty girl."

Please, please, please do.

He slipped the other shoe on and secured it with a nice rub up and down her ankle and the front of her foot. "Does it feel good?"

"More than you know. I mean—

"I already know what you mean, sugar. It can feel a whole lot better if you'll let it."

Normally when a salesman said that to her, he was referring to comfort pads. Not that day. The comfort was definitely in the slide.

"Would you like to stand on them, walk around, get your feet wet from the comfort of pure fine Italian leather?"

She stared down at him, lips barely parted, eyes narrowing in a sultry way. "I don't think I can."

His lips moved closer to her ear. "Tell me why not."

"I can't. It's too embarrassing. Suppose your coworker comes out."

"Then he'll just have to see the same thing I do—a lovely

young lady wearing a pair of red pumps that can make dicks rocket up to the sky."

She slowly looked at the front of his pants and saw a protrusion she'd only dreamed of; she wanted to hold all hot, hard, nine-plus inches of him within her small warm hand. She knew he had to be at least nine inches from the looks of him. Any man that damn pretty had to have one the length of the Pacific, and just as deep.

His voice took control of her again. "I hope it's everything you want it to be."

"From what I can see, it's more than enough to reach my Milky Way." She stood and walked around the carpet, raising her pants legs above the knee. One step on the cushiony leather insole and she was hooked. Though she couldn't determine if the feel was from the shoes themselves or the salesman. She wanted to think it was purely the shoes but knew a feeling like that came from only one source—a man so damn gorgeous that she failed to see straight. Hopefully she'd be able to walk without him knowing exactly how insane she was over the idea of him deeply inside her tight, sweet sex.

She bounced on her toes a bit and walked around a tad more, knowing his eyes were on how juicy her butt looked in those tight jeans. Tight jeans and a pair of heels always did it for a man, and knowing that was what made her wear her tightest jeans. She wanted his erection to cry out for her, squirm so hard within his pants that he'd bust completely out, find his way into her hands, and get sucked the rest of the afternoon. Only three problems with her plan: her mother, her sister and his coworker. She turned, walked back to him. "I like these. They're hot!"

"Yes, ma'am, they certainly are."

For Jason, watching Amber walk around nearly killed him. She was beautiful, absolutely stunning, and she had legs like a fashion model. The shoes weren't doing it—it was all her. True, heels always accentuated the curve of a woman's legs, but hers needed no help. She'd have looked perfect in sand-covered beach thongs as far as he was concerned. That was something else he wouldn't mind seeing her in—bikini thongs, just bikini thongs, and nothing but that! Given where they were, he had to settle for the real and anything his imagination could allow. He let his mind to go crazy, along with his crotch, which, by the way, was an inch away from the stars.

"They do look incredible. Is there anything else I can do for you, Amber Marie Donohue? Because believe me, I can do a lot."

"You've done enough."

"Not really. You haven't told me how it, I mean they, feel on you."

"You really want to know?"

"Look at my pants again, beautiful."

No more hesitation on her part; she couldn't help but look at something she knew was tempting. He was large and thick. She could see that much through his pants. He definitely had everything her body ached for. Quickly she had to get her mind from how many inches she knew he had and return it to something sane—shoes. That idea worked all too briefly since she really couldn't keep her mind from his pants. "They feel incredible, nice and snug, tight where they need to be, loose and languid everywhere else. I could have more and more of them."

"I would love that. Sliding something warm and tight into you would be a man's dream come true. Speaking of such, where's your shop? I have lunch in an hour, and we could do more than eat."

The idea of being his lunch, or at least eating with him, stirred feminine hormones like crazy. Then reality came back, and with a vengeance. "My mom and sister are here with me."

"That could be sticky. Where's the shop, anyway? Maybe I can come by late one night and slide something else onto that succulent body of yours."

"What would you have in mind?"

He looked around at the empty store and the even emptier hallway in front of the store, then took her hand. With her small hand wrapped in his, he stood and smoothed it up and down a bulging zipper. He was on fire and was so ready for her to feel his heat, his desire. It felt so damn good as she laced her fingers around that tight, lengthy bulge, soothing its burning desire. Her hand found his juicy tip, delicately pinched it, feeling it quiver at her touch, massaging his contours, making him grow within her hand, a hand that could barely handle such a large shaft.

Had he not been the gentleman he was, he would have lost it, then and there. His other hand covered hers, pressing it harder yet gently against an erection that was climbing the damn walls. His voice lowered. "Feel good to you, sweetheart?"

She continued to feel his thickness, his mass, wanted to toy with it more, stretch it, taste it over and over again until she got him to cream. Her soft reply said it all. "It's incredible."

"Just incredible?"

"Juicy!"

"Getting closer. Keep going with those words, girl, 'cause I love how it sounds."

"Jason, if I told you what you were doing to my nerve endings, I'd embarrass you to tears."

"I'll cry for a sexy woman any day. Just say the word."

Her legs became so weak from wanting him that she had to sit down. He met her on the floor, slowly bending on one knee due to the arousal between his thighs. He then remembered who he was and what he was supposed to be doing—selling shoes. "I hope I wasn't too forward with you, Amber. I just get carried away in the presence of a diamond-studded queen."

"Everything is perfect about you, Jason DeMaras, every single inch. And I love compliments, so keep them coming. I need them."

He gazed into her eyes once more, wanting, wishing, hoping the store would go away and leave the two of them to disappear into a sexual haven, never to be disturbed again. However, the heavy clunking of a window-shopper's shoes brought him back, though his eyes never left hers.

Amber was the one who had to clear the air. "I'd better have you get these to the register before you make me embarrass both of us, Mr. Jason."

"I like how you said that. I'd love to be embarrassed by you. By the way, there isn't a Mr. Donohue, is there? I forgot to ask you the other day."

"No, there isn't; not anymore. Maurice and I have been history for almost two years."

"And no one else snatched you? Incredible."

"I went through a period where I didn't want to be snatched. Dealing with a breakup is hard on a girl's heart."

"What about being snatched now? Is that possible?"

"Could be. Depends on who the thief is."

"Well, me?"

"I'm as good as stolen, then. But, first and foremost, is there a Mrs. Jason DeMaras?"

His eyes rolled in a bit of skepticism. "There was a Mrs. DeMaras, but we're divorced. We recently got back together but didn't renew our vows." He saw the saddened look on her face and quickly jumped to the punch line. "I'm getting out of it again because it's not working. I did it for the sake of my son, but some things are never meant to be. Then there are those that are." He eyed her seductively.

"Are you sure?"

"Surer than sure."

Amber reached into her purse and handed him her business card. "Take this and call me. Anytime."

"Like tonight?"

"Like whenever."

His smile lit the place again. "Cool." Then he looked over at the unopened box of shoes. "The navy blue ones would look just as good on you. Wanna try them on?"

"I don't think I'd survive it. You're a heck of a salesman, and I'd walk out of here with way too many shoes I can't afford."

"You'll survive it; take my word for it. And, no, I won't let Amber go broke. You still haven't told me where your store is, though."

"Main and Fifteen Mile Road."

"Just up the street, and a slip-slide away, beautiful. When can I come by?"

"When do you want to?"

"Tomorrow night, around eight?"

"Perfect. I'll have the pictures ready, and a few other things."

"Sounds like a hell of a plan. Pictures, though?"

"Yeah, you know. I told you I'd have pictures of the jewelry. Do you still want to show them off here?"

"Sure, they're lovely. I was hoping the pictures would be of you, though, all hot and iced down, dripping wet for me."

"I'm already dripping wet for you. As we speak, my panties are jacked . . . sliding across a slick crotch! You did that just by touching me."

"I'd love to do more than that."

"You may just get that chance. You'd have to take *those* pictures, though."

"Gladly, and if you think your panties are jacked, I have to get rid of a hard-on. Care to help with that?"

"I'd love to."

"Really?"

"If you're anything like what I felt a minute ago, I'd be crazy not to take advantage of an offer like that, but what would you think of me?"

"I'd think you're the best thing that has ever happened to me."

At that, he slid the pumps from her feet, gently tickled the underside of her perfectly painted pink toes, and enjoyed her squirming. "I like how you move, would love to see more of that."

"I just can't believe you think I'm pretty."

"I didn't say you were pretty. I said you were beautiful, and I'd like to see if it covers the entire range."

Malcolm stepped from the back. "Think you can handle the store a while I get coffee? Inventory is hell, man."

That lit both Jason and Amber's eyes. Jason barely got to his feet due to the pressure in his pants. "Sure, man. It's your break time, anyway."

They watched Malcolm leave; then Jason took her hand. "What time is your mother due to come in?"

"Don't worry about them. Kitchen utensils are what they live for, though neither can boil an egg. Go figure."

"I'd rather steal a minute or two in the back corner with you. Care to indulge me?" He took her hand into his and pulled her along. "Don't worry; it's all good, and your reputation will be spotless. Trust me."

Being pulled into Jason's lair was the only thing Amber cared about. Screw reputations. What she wanted *was* a good screw. Before she could say a word, his lips delicately tasted hers, nibbling at first, then becoming more forceful. The feel of her lips against his tongue teased him, pulled him in directions he hadn't been in all of his thirty years of living and loving. This was loving and living, everything he had been denied until Amber Marie walked into his store and set his pants on fire.

He pressed her wriggling body into his, feeling her, kissing soft-as-a-petal skin and relishing in it. Her breasts meshed against his body so seductively, making his erection seemingly span miles, and all he wanted was her hands around it, stroking it much the way she was kissing his lips.

Amber never knew a man could make her so hungry. That's what she was—hungry for him, hungry for his thick cock to press up against her pliable body. Her hips rocked with his, feeling white fire raging between her thighs the more he squeezed her behind. The more he stroked her, the more wild and ravenous she became kissing him. Had anything ever tasted that good to her? Was anything allowed to taste like that without being illegal? The fuck she knew, all she wanted was more of what she was getting.

Their hips rocked in unison as Jason pressed her into the wall, touching and squeezing everything he could get his hands on. And when he slid his fingers between her legs, she gladly parted, letting him rub the jeans material against an already electrified clit. He stroked her like they were actually making it. Amber wondered why he should have all the fun. One hand found his zipper and rubbed it until the metal burned her skin; then she slid the zipper down. She reached inside. There it was! He was so hot and hard, so ready to be sucked dry. She reached within his underwear and fondled what she thought she'd never have the chance to really see and feel.

He parted from her by barely inches to let her see what she had unearthed. There he stood to her, a tip so smooth and soft, glistening with droplets of joy. Her hands surrounded him, jerked him vigorously up and down as he watched. She wanted to taste it so bad, have it fill her mouth and stroke her throat until he gave, but with her luck, someone would walk in and interrupt. It would kill her having to pull away from a cock that beautiful, stiff, and full of semen. Besides, he'd lose his job. Couldn't have that, so she settled for getting him off with an erotic hand job.

She continued kissing his lips until her own were swollen, and she continued laying it on thick between his thighs. She pumped that delicious weapon until he felt the rush coming. He grabbed a few sheets of tissue and prepared himself for what would soon erupt. And as he spilled into the tissue, his frantic hands stroked the inside seam of her now wet jeans. "God, this is incredible, Amber. I didn't know anyone could make me spill like this. Is it good for you, girl?"

She couldn't speak until her own monstrous orgasm stopped rattling her body. Once her fitful body calmed, she smiled into his satisfied face. "My God, it was everything I wanted it to be; it was just over too soon."

"I can take care of that as soon as you let me."

She cleaned his still-hard member and tried zipping his pants but needed his help. In another minute, they looked respectable again. But before she could give him a definite time, the entrance bell chimed and in stepped her mother and sister. Perfect timing.

She could always count on her mother to be gauche and disgusting.

"There's my baby." She looked over at Jason holding the shoeboxes. "Did my little girl make you take out all your goodies?"

"Yes, she did, but I didn't mind a bit." The goodies she was talking about and the goodies he delivered were two entirely different things. But he kept his mouth shut.

Mrs. Donohue rambled on. "She's definitely a shoe connoisseur."

Amber stopped her mother before Jason was turned off, making him wonder if she'd be the same way in thirty years. "I'm buying the red pair, Mother, and, no, I didn't make him take out his goodies." *Not all of them; just the best one.*

Geneva sat next to her, lowering her voice. "Girl, his ass is fine. You need to jump on that."

Amber smiled at Jason as he walked away with the boxes. "What makes you think I haven't?"

3

oh, what a night

That night, Amber fell asleep with the box of red shoes at her side and Jason's card in her hand as the distant thunder lulled her. She hoped Jason was serious and not simply trying to entice her into the navy pair of Meuccis, which were way too expensive for her Dooney & Burke purse (which would have been another three hundred dollars had she not gone to a street vendor in Manhattan two years ago).

Her days of the fly guys were over. She wanted something true, meaningful. Her dilemma with relationships centered on her actions. In the past, she'd always been too free, giving it up way too soon and way too much. That was the last thing she wanted happening with Jason, if there was going to be a relationship in the first place. That, she didn't know, after the hand job she'd already provided. The thing about it, Jason was the kind of man who made women want to give it up. One look into his mysterious eyes would seriously make a woman strip on the premises. Imagining his lips on hers . . . well, the idea of it alone made her groin muscles constrict with outrageous spasms.

As she tossed and turned in her bed, punching her pillow to the absolute right consistency, she wondered if she had the strength to resist Jason long enough to build a relationship, or if she would let it all hang out the minute he touched her in close quarters—like her unoccupied store. Could be risky.

She was too old for that—too old and too lonely. Time to make moves, the right moves, and possibly start over with Jason by leaving his cock in his pants. *Could it happen?*

On the morning in question, Amber awakened to terrible thunder and lightning, splitting the sky and making the world dark and gloomy, like that old TV show *Dark Shadows*. She slowly pulled back the covers, hoping not to see Barnabas Collins standing at the foot of her bed. Instead, what greeted her were rain-slicked windows, drenching the streets and her Honda; she was surprised that the thunder hadn't set off the car alarm. What alarmed her even more was the forecast coming from her clock radio. Thunderstorms expected for the majority of the day and into the evening, huh? She hoped it wouldn't dampen her plans with Jason that night, if he came at all.

She had to prove something to herself that night—would she be able to hold her emotions at bay and not go all the way with Jason, or would she let loose, explore all his possibilities, and pray he'd call her back one day?

By eight-thirty that night, the rain was still falling, but through it all, her mind's-eye saw Jason smiling at her, making his seductive moves across her body and taking her to paradise. Only thoughts of him could keep her mind from the terrible weather. Running from the car to her shop drenched her from head to toe. She was, at least, thankful that she'd brought a change of clothing, along with the red stilettos, newly purchased thanks to Jason DeMaras.

In the middle of changing from her jeans and T-shirt, she heard a loud noise coming from her stock room. With the jeans barely hovering on her delicate hips, she went to see. Part of the roof had caved in from the heavy rain and water was flooding the floor. Quickly, she moved away from the constant flow and stumbled backward into Jason's arms. He took her by the hips, balancing her so she wouldn't fall. The minute she looked into his eyes, she couldn't help but smile. "Jason! I didn't expect to see you for another half-hour."

"I couldn't wait. Hope that's okay with you, and by the looks of things, I couldn't have been more on time. What's going on here?"

She pointed up. "A bad patch job, considering the money I paid."

"Then they'll have to redo it. The rest of the shop is beautiful, though. I walked around a bit looking for you. Your display windows are nice and roomy; enough space to really put on a jewelry extravaganza."

She smiled at his profile as his eyes scanned the room. "That was the selling point, the windows."

With his eyes still astray, staring at the hole in the ceiling, he uttered, "I also noticed the buttery-soft leather couch in the main room." As he faced her, he pulled her closer, steadying her as the water wet the bottoms of their shoes. His face was now barely inches from hers, so close that even in the dark he could see hints of her lipstick, a cognac red, and irresistible. Though he liked the hue, all he wanted to do was suck it off in a wet and wild feeding frenzy and continue what they started the other day. Along with that, her scent enthralled him, reminding him of a field of lilacs but with a punch of sexuality added. Suddenly, what was going on with her roof was of no importance; there was just her—how she smiled at him, how her body molded to his upon contact.

Amber was nothing more than putty, ready to be molded and stretched into any position he wanted her to be in. She could barely talk. "You really like my spot?"

"Every spot you own, girl. If only I could feel it, really feel it, without those jeans covering it."

"What I meant was—"

"I know what you meant, and I know what's on my mind."

No! This can't happen so soon. What about a relation-

ship? What about a first date even? She was being pulled into a direction she wanted to be in, yet didn't want to be in, at least not that night.

Well, maybe that night.

Pulling away from the likes of him would be torture. They both really did want the same thing and right away, despite what her superego was trying to dictate. What had to happen to clear her head was meaningless chatter, something to take his mind from the front of his pants. "My opening is in a month, and I don't want any more unexpected problems with this damn roof."

"I understand. Openings mean big business." He scanned her clothing, not expecting to see her in jeans and a damp T-shirt, but the sight of it invigorated every part of his male anatomy, making him harder, wetter. The idea of her body so close to his wasn't helping the situation because he could feel her. The way her breasts pressed against his chest sent his mind out in orbit. The way her hips felt against his hands made him sweat. The way she looked in those tight jeans and soggy shirt got his juices flowing, and the only thing he could think of was tasting her, every part of her, from her hair to her painted pink toenails.

His first plan was to back off, take things slow even though he was on fire for her. He really wanted something to work for him in the romance department, but she was killing him with the vibes from hell, and he got caught in the pit. Before he realized what was happening, he heard his own words, husky words, excited, anticipated words. "What the hell are you doing to me, Amber?"

She looked down at herself, noticing she was still in her work clothes. That was the last thing she wanted to be in on his arrival. Her idea of greeting him in a grand way would be wearing a red and silver strapless dress, silver and red crystal earrings, the new shoes, and make-up. Something always seemed to ruin her plans.

She stepped away from him, though hating to move one

iota away, and rubbed her palms against the wet shirt. "Sorry. I planned to have my dress and make-up on by now. I'll change in the—

"Don't! I like what I see right now; sexy beyond reason."

"This crap! Come on, Jason, I look and smell like I've been working all day. This is not how I wanted to prepare myself for you. This is your first time in my store, and I wanted it to be special. There's hardly any lights on in here for you to really see the place."

"I see what I want, Amber, and take my word for it, the jeans are on jam." He spied hints of dark, raised nipples poking from her shirt. "The wet shirt is even better. Shows what I've been tasting in my dreams." His thumb rubbed against the plump bud. "Yum! I like the dark, anyway; makes for better romance. Don't you agree?"

Where was her mind going? she wondered. Was she going to let him swoon her into the sack or do what she knew was the best thing and move away? Doing the best thing was always hard for her, and not as fun. Sure, she wanted to take things slow with him, but he made that terribly hard. He looked so good in the semi dark. Barely visible hints of light from outside flashed against his body, lighting him up like a birthday cake—one that she wanted to lick the icing from.

There that damn ego was, mentally telling her to keep her distance, though that was the last thing her body wanted to do. Instead of answering his question, she moved around the situation, or at least tried to. She delivered a giddy laugh, saying. "You mentioned you have a son. How old is he?"

"I don't want to talk about my son. I don't even want to discuss you. I want—need—to know what you feel like. I wanna feel my body inside of yours, feel you constricting around me, calling me, tasting me. I want it, Amber, and I think you do, too, if you don't mind the boldness of my statement. Is it true, though? Do you want me?"

Their eyes locked as she searched for a reasonable response, but there wasn't one when it came to him. With him, reason was merely a mind trick, something not fathomable. What was left to deal with was the id, that instinctual feeling-reaction part of everyone's inner self that reacted to sheer pleasure. The id was slowly taking over, telling her in that devilish little voice, "*Go for it, live a little. So what if you may never see him again after this night? The sex will be so worth it.* The voice had a point, but she wanted Jason for more than a night. She settled for pleasing both the id and the ego, going for it in hopes that she'd still see him again.

Her lips barely inches from his, she breathed out her last sentence before total seduction took over. "I do want you, Jason, but for more than this night. Is that possible?"

"Anything is. And I swear I'll be so damn good to you. You'll beg me to leave you alone." He gently nibbled her bottom lip with slow, sensual licks, then conquered her upper lip much the same way but with more elaborate kisses, over and over again. From there, he made the journey to her neck, licking a path from her earlobe to her collarbone. She smelled so wonderful, and the more he kissed each tender spot on her neck, the better her aroma was to his senses. The tenting in his pants practically drove a wedge between them, but that was the feeling he wanted to achieve. The minute he laid eyes on her weeks before, he knew nothing would do other than being wrapped around her in every possible sexual position. It had to start that night, in the dark, in a closed storeroom in the middle of a storm—damaged ceiling and all.

Amber couldn't break the trance. Nothing she tried could make her move away from him. He felt as good as he looked and tasted even better. Her hands roamed up and down his dampened silk shirt, feeling tight muscles, ripples, the broadness of his upper back, which tapered to the smallness of his waist. His side muscles hardened with each stroke she adorned him with, making him react to her tender touch as she tickled him by grazing fingernails up and down his torso. The more she lovingly tickled him, the more his lips sucked hers.

His tongue entered her parted lips, making his home there

as he eagerly clawed at her clothing. A tricky hand found the hem of her shirt and raised it, grazing her warm flesh. Soon his other hand followed; she broke their kiss temporarily to raise the shirt over her head and snap her bra open. Their lips met again in a lush, languid type of contact. Delicate skin graced his palms and fingertips, a feeling he'd never before experienced, and it crushed him, made him weak to the very touch of her hot satin skin. He had to have her.

For better leverage, he leaned against the wall, sliding her jeans zipper down and quickly reaching to finger the frilly seat of her panties, wanting what was inside, aching for it. He wanted to drown in her nectar, feel it against his fingers, and eat the place from which it came. The idea of it made him take her into his arms and find that leather-clad sofa again. With speed in his step and wild desire, he found the sofa and practically floated in the air to it.

Once in front of it, he immediately slid the jeans down her legs, removing her feet from the narrow legs and slid her sandals from her feet. That wasn't enough though. He had to scan the package from top to bottom, taking in all she had to offer.

And she let him!

His first move was to breasts burning for want of his touch. After another sweet kiss, he fingered each hardened bud, smoothing the pad of his thumb against each one. "Jesus, Amber." The words barely out of his mouth, he sucked one nipple, licking in circles while massaging the other. He gave equal attention to the other. From that point on, his track across her body started at those delectable nipples, sucking hard on them before moving down, darting his tongue in and out of a delicate navel. He kissed all the way down to the entrance of the golden palace. Immediately his fingers dipped into the front of the lacy garment, feeling feather light hair brushing across his hot fingers.

There was no going back for either of them. For Amber, the anticipation of finally feeling this man inside her, any way he could get inside, controlled her. Feeling her panties being removed brought on the tightest grind within her core, one that almost flattened her. He hadn't even entered before she had a mind-blowing orgasm that left her speechless.

"Don't go there yet, baby. Let me feel it when you come. There's nothing more exciting than having a woman you adore boil over inside because of you."

"Too late for that."

"No way. There's more, take my word for it." He helped her step from the panties, then began again. Fingers that she ached to have inside her invaded her one by one, slipping inside her moistness. The entrance of his third finger melted her, allowing her to be totally free to surrender to the pleasures only Jason could give her. Rhythm and friction together electrified her, sending pulsing waves up and down her body as he moved deeper inside her, fingering a slick, warm clit ready to vibrate against him. A combination of his fingers working magic inside her and the awesome power of the hard-on splitting his zipper made her caress him more, call out to him, work up and down against that fabulous erection. Her only wish was that his zipper would just vanish, go away and never return again. She wanted to feel the power firsthand . . . and in each hand. God only knew he had enough to fill both hands at the same time. She wanted to know how much and for how long.

As though reading her mind, he broke the kiss, staring into a face so wonderfully flushed that he thought he would come from the mere sight of her pleasure. He kissed her fingers, whispering, "Let me take it, baby. Let me take it long and hard, all night, all day tomorrow. Let me live within all that juicy smoothness you possess."

Without waiting for a response, he laid her bare body on the sofa and stared. "You're the most beautiful thing I've ever seen or ever will see again. If I don't get you, I'll bust."

"Not on my showroom floor you won't. I want your best, Jason, and your best can't spill anywhere but inside of me."

When his lips kissed her mound, she bucked, but he held her in place. "Not yet, baby, but soon." He bent her knees and moved in between them, eating and catching every ounce of fluid spilling from her. Her aroma was unimaginable, and the more he ate her, making her back arch to the sky, the more he wanted.

In the middle of his taste-fest, he heard her whimpers, calling to him, watched as she grabbed her breasts in heightened eroticism. He squirmed as that tiny part of her vibrated against his tongue. That's when he knew for sure he had to have it, all of it, every single drop of her sweet nectar.

In one swift motion, he stood and removed his belt, letting it drop to the floor with a thud. Then Amber stood, in a hurry to unearth his treasures. "It's my turn." Quickly she unbuttoned the shirt, seeing hints of his dark skin underneath. Her fingers trembled from the thought of seeing his bare chest and licking everything in sight. In dire haste, his shirt was off his shoulders and down his arms. Her lips went to his left nipple, feeling the rough hardness of his skin against the soft surface of her tongue. Over and over, around and down to a raised navel that simply took her taste buds to the edge of temptation. She licked it, tickling its center and loving how his stomach quivered. His head reared back, taking in all she delivered. "Take it, girl, fucking do me in!"

Not just words—the moment of truth; hard, sexual truth.

She had never felt desire before. She thought she had, but compared to Jason, her other lovers were mere inexperienced teens. He hadn't even entered her yet and she was knocking on heaven's door. He quickly stepped out of his pants while kicking his leather crocs aside. Once he was almost nude, she stepped back to marvel at her prize. Her eyes widened at the sight of his clothed erection. "This can't be real."

He moved into her again. "More real than life itself. Take it, Amber; feel it, experience it, and let it move any mountain you may have."

As if fire was burning her hands, she reached within those Jockeys and felt all of her wildest dreams; ten plus inches of hulking, squirming meat, ready to devour anything in its path, and she couldn't wait to have it. She could hardly believe the touch of a man's erection could take her there. Then again, Jason wasn't just a man; he was *the* man, the only man who could sweet-talk his way right into her tight, wet, quivering spot, and she was ready to give it up.

He sat on the sofa, feeling the soft buttery leather against his wet body, then spread his legs for her. "Bend to me and taste. Let me into your mouth and hands." He took her hand and pulled her closer. "You're the writer, now write your book. I'm every blank page you'll ever need."

Her story started. The minute his warm, plump flesh met her lips, her story was written, and he was the hero. Moment after moment, her lips seduced him, teased him, manipulated him to the point where he thought he'd break. Simply pleasing this wonderful man was all she wanted to do.

Amber's assault took him to his breaking point as he felt her lips around an erection that surpassed all space and time. Her teasing tongue played with his mushroomed tip, darting in and out of its center, raking her nails against his scrotum. His back arched, forcing more of him against her wanton lips. Amber took all he gave her and asked yet for more. He willingly gave until he felt he'd soak everything in the immediate vicinity.

Watching her devour half his length with smooth, even strokes excited him way beyond what any woman ever did to him in the past. No one had taken him to the peak of the mountain and pushed him over, until Amber appeared on the horizon. She was what he wanted, what he really wanted. What was so special about Amber? Her looks were hotter than flaming coals; her touch was softer than satin, but that wasn't it. She was so perfect and smart. Smart women turned his lights completely on. Amber was her own woman, but with a touch of insecurity. That was the sexy part. That's what made him want her more, to cure that insecurity and make her understand she was a true queen.

He pulled back from her, quickly brushing his lips against hers once again. "It's time, baby." He patted his thighs and helped her as she straddled him. Positioning her barely inches above his tight, pulsing length. "It's all yours. Take it and ride me until there's nothing left on the planet but you and I."

Poetic words made her skin hot and cold at the same time, shivering to the idea of Jason DeMaras directly before her. "There is nothing on the planet but us, Jason." Barely able to speak from wanting him, she slowly inched down upon a massive shaft. Her body widened to him, accommodated him, stretched to the limits for him until he filled her to capacity. Once she met the base of his power, she rode him, pumped up and down on him as he teased each breast again, licking and sucking to her rhythm, in unison.

His powerful thrusts nailed her, pumped into her tiny frame; yet it was a frame strong enough to withstand the vibrant thrusts of a long-awaited lover. The fact that the prettiest man in the world was inside of her made her pulse and heart quicken, crying out to him, calling, begging for more of him. Facing him as he vigorously pumped deeper and deeper into her diamond mine wasn't enough. She had to look up at him, see him on top of her, make him move the sofa across the room from their lovemaking. Her breathy tone made him immediately do what was asked. "I wanna be on my back, Jason, staring up at you, having your sweat drip onto me, have you bust me wide open."

Tenderly and delicately, Jason shifted, landing Amber exactly where she wanted to be—on her back with her thighs to the sky. One look at him staring down at her and she came, bubbled over and tightened around him as though she were an anaconda taking her prey. The deeper he went, the tighter and deeper she took him.

Amber rocked to his exaggerated rhythm for what seemed

to be hours on end. Looking up and seeing him jerk, convulse, and sweat against her made the river overflow. She came again, yelling his name, clawing his back and hips with tender rakes, making him rock harder and harder until the sofa did move. It was either the sofa or the earth; she didn't give a damn which one it was.

Hearing Amber call to him started his chain reaction. He quickly pulled out and unloaded everywhere, spurting thrusts that, again, made her weak to him. The sight of him coming brought on her fifth orgasm, a record for her considering who she had been with before.

Jason was the king, and she had been royally crowned.

Amber pumped his still-taut phallus, making sure every drop he owned . . . owned her. His intense stare and husky, sexed-out voice taunted her. "That's right, girl, keep rocking it, control it, make it drip again. More, Amber. Work it!" The second ultimate release. "Amberrr!"

Did she stop after he was seemingly devastated? Hell no! Her vigorous hand strokes ignited him again, pumping more and more of his liquid sugar into the palms of her hands. He was warm, sweet and gooey, heaven on earth.

He collapsed on top of her, panting, heaving, but managing to speak. "That was the best damn sex I've ever had." He slowly faced her, staring into a still flushed, excited, yet calm face. "Girl, you are it! I've never been that crazy before while making love. I've never wanted to. What have you done to me?"

"Everything good."

"Damn straight!" He laid against her again and they both were silent.

An hour later, a clap of thunder awakened them. He jumped and looked out of the window at the milky blue and lavender sky, seeing that the rain had ceased despite the thunder. He stroked her cheeks. "Can I stay here with you tonight?"

"Definitely. I need you to be my blanket."

"Can I see you again tomorrow night?"

Exactly what she wanted and prayed she'd hear. "Same time, same station?"

"Cute! Anything Amber wants, Amber gets."

They fell asleep, one-on-one.

4

scotch and absolut, a perfect match

One week later.

Meeting Jason in a leaky storefront with construction workers crawling all over the place wasn't happening. Where would the closeness be? What about the eroticism? Thankfully for Amber, there was always a plan B—meeting Jason in front of the Lilly Ruben Salon at Somerset.

She knew it wasn't his night to work late, having called and rescheduled their next rendezvous. As usual, she wanted to look spectacular for him. Though in his eyes, Amber Marie Donohue could say, do, or wear no evil, all five-foot-six inches of her.

For Jason, every minute working with even the faintest idea of her being in the mall somewhere was setting his nerve endings aflame. That's why they decided on her meeting him at another store instead at his. Any woman other than Amber who strutted in there for shoes was just out of fucking luck if Jason's eyes met with Amber's.

However, they remained less than worlds apart since the salon was almost across the way from Roma Shoes, and Jason caught a side glance at her; she looked fantastic in a pair of red leather, skintight pants, red heels and a flowery red and yellow lacy blouse. Naturally, the signature V-neck was there to arouse anything on him that wasn't already sky-high. She had that knack. Jason could smell the sex in the air and couldn't wait to take flight into her jet stream. Someone with her sex appeal had sexual aromas circling her head in waves of passion, and Jason, well, he simply wanted to be her pilot.

The minute the last customer left, so did Jason, leaving two of his coworkers there to pick up the slack. He seemingly floated across the aisle, smiling as he approached, taking her hands into his. "As I live and breathe, the original Helen Blazes."

They shared a brief kiss.

Amber, hating to break the kiss, realized where they were. The place was still on jam at almost nine at night. She stared into his wonderfully exotic face. "Now, tell me who the heck Helen Blazes is."

"Someone that's so hot the flames dance around her, vibrate around her, mix and mingle with every essence of her persona. And that red really sets you off."

"Glad to accommodate you."

"And you do it so well. All I have to do is close my eyes and you're there."

"I'm here now, and thankfully you are, too."

"I'm always going to be here, Amber, especially now."

He glanced at the last-minute shoppers who were doing everything in their power to hit the rest of the stores in the remaining twenty minutes before closing time. He said in a rushed voice, "Let's get outta here."

A quirky smile brightened her face. "Anything in mind?"

"You betcha!"

Where they went wasn't exactly what she was expecting. He selected a cozy, out-of-the-way club a few miles from the mall called Innuendos. Amber loved the sound of it but preferred sipping amaretto by his fireplace—better yet, in his bed.

They selected a nice secluded table that was deep, dark, and in the back where no one but the waitress saw them. Amber ordered an Absolut Vanilla on the rocks. For him, a scotch and soda, a man's-man drink!

He smiled at her choice of beverage. "You sure you can handle Mr. Absolut? It is vodka, you know."

"This is a rare occasion for me, so I figured I'd go all the way live tonight."

"Like last night?"

"Absolut-ly." Suddenly, as if second-guessing her behavior the evening before, a bit of skepticism filled her mind. "Do you think I've been too forward? I mean, after all, we're still new to one another."

"Have you been enjoying it?"

"Do I look like I've been enjoying it?"

"You look like you were born to do it, with me, and it's been out of this fucking world."

"But how do you feel now about making love to me?"

"That's exactly what it was, Amber, making love. For me, it wasn't just sex. Like I said before, I don't know what it is about you, but I had to have you, and I still do."

Their drinks came, but Jason's eyes never left Amber's; he simply reached for his drink while getting an eyeful of her. "A better way to put it—if this wasn't a public place, I'd be on top of you right now." He swallowed hard, setting his glass down. "Don't ever think you're too wayward for me. I like it wild and crazy, and the more I see you, the wilder I want sex with you to get."

"Then I'm not just a fling?"

"I'm still here, aren't I?"

"Most definitely, and, baby, the view is fine."

He finished the rest of his drink in one gulp. "Glad someone thinks so."

Amber detected the sudden ambivalence. "What do you mean?"

"What I mean is that not everyone has the free mind you have. I admire that about you."

"What happened today? Jason, you know you can tell me."

"Gina happened. My ex. She's making it hard to see my

son, saying I suddenly skipped out on her and Keith. That's not what I did. She and I shouldn't have gotten back together because I knew it wouldn't last—it can't with someone like her."

"What's she like?"

"Self-absorbed, into whatever money she can get from me and spending it all on herself. She says it's in Keith's best interest, but she doesn't spend anything on him. I do!"

"Well, I guess that answers the question I wanted to ask."

"Really? What?"

"What's it like to be married. I've been alone for thirty-two years, and I'd actually like to give it a try one day."

"The previous men in your life were crazy. I'm so shocked that you haven't been snatched—well, not counting by me. If you'll let me, I'd be glad to take up the slack from those poor dopes who were too stupid to take advantage of a good thing."

She slid her empty glass aside. "That's just it. Maybe I was too much of a good thing before, giving myself too freely and being left in the dust. That's why I was wondering about my actions with you. I don't want to turn you off."

"Girl, that's the last thing you could ever do. The thing about it, you're so different. You made me want everything you have, right away and to savor for years to come."

"So you'd try another relationship again?"

"Yes, definitely. But only with you." His hand slid up and down her leather pants, slowly, softly. "Just by knowing you a few weeks, you make me want what my parents have—forty years of nothin' but love. They had their ups and downs like everyone, but basically they loved each other enough to have four kids."

"And where are you in that line up?"

"Second. There's Jane, myself, James, and my baby brother, Justin."

"All *J*s. But what about Keith? Shouldn't he have been named after the sexiest man I've ever seen?"

"Well, if you're referring to me, which I hope you are, then I was just unlucky enough not to have my own son named after me. My daughter, Justine, did get the J. She has a different mother than Keith. I guess both he and I are unlucky."

"Actually, I think Gina is the unlucky one. She doesn't know a good life when she sees one." She leaned over and delivered a delectable nibble across his bottom lip, then slowly pulled away. "Umm, if I keep that up, you may very well get your Jason Jr."

"Don't stop the flow, girl." He leaned into her, sliding the tip of his tongue into her willing mouth, savoring her, physically crying out to do more, yet keeping it to a low moan. "You are really something, Ms. Amber Donohue, and you smell so good, natural."

"Do I smell good enough to dance with? Phyllis Hyman's "Be One" is playing in the background. Hear it?"

"Isn't it just like you to know a romantic tune when you hear it?"

"Not exactly. It's from *School Daze*. I'm a big Spike Lee fan."

"And I'm a big Amber Marie fan." He took her hand, bringing her to her feet. "That song sounds too good not to be sliding against you to it. Hold me tight and I'll make the world disappear for us."

"It already has."

Mood music; that was exactly what Phyllis Hyman filled the club with and was exactly what Amber wanted. Having not gotten her fill of him the night before, she capitalized on the opportunity to be close to him again, slowly, methodically, as Jason's body gently pressed against hers. Her arms encircled his shoulders, lacing her fingers around his neck. She relished the fact that he was already sweating for her, from her.

Her cheek pressed intimately against his, feeling his moist, warm flesh, remembering how hot and satisfying he was to her last night—awesome, a feeling never to forget as long as she lived on the face of the earth. The fact was he was so unconsciously wonderful to her; so sexual and intimate in an embrace that her clothing began to cling mercilessly to her. Her only thought was reliving their lovemaking right there on the dance floor, feeling his body as it swayed against hers in rhythmic vibes. No man before him got her to the point where she'd be a fool for him. Hell, she knew she fell fast for men, but this was something different, something new and exciting, and she wanted it to continue into future lives, whatever they would be.

As his hips continued to sway and move her practically into an orgasmic bliss, she could feel the very tool that could take her there, a colossus of an erection wanting, needing, trying to satisfy her every which way. The only words for that kind of assault were *pleasurable torture*. An orgasm shot through her so fast that it made her tremble, edging her to stretch her arms tighter around his shoulders.

Her reaction didn't go unnoticed. He loved how her body molded to his, reacted to him, accepting his pressure. "You okay, baby?"

She looked into a face barely visible by the sultry nightclub hues, feeling his words as he spoke. "I'm fine."

"I know that already. Your body tells me everything I need to know. Was it a good one for you?"

Yes, he knew exactly the response he forced from her, and telling him a lie would be as see-through as glass. "Every time you touch me I do that."

Needing to know, hear, and feel more, he pulled her closer, whispering against her crystal-clad lobe, "Then let me do more. No one will know what we're doing. They're too into Ms. Phyllis to give a good damn about us."

"No way. They'll have to mop up what's left of me."

He briefly kissed her lips. "Those words, girl. You can make a man come just by talking to him, let alone touching him."

"That was my plan from day one."

"It worked."

He swayed her pliable body to yet another song from the *School Daze* soundtrack, "The Perfect Match." That's what they were, and they bonded tighter together than cement. The way her body moved delicately against his shaft tantalized him, made him harder, thicker, juicier; so tight and stiff within her presence that he had to back off. "If we don't sit down, you won't be the only thing they'll have to mop up."

Amber reached between his thighs and palmed him, acknowledging his obvious pleasure. "Making love is so real with you; more real than life itself."

"It is life; life pumping out of me and into you. The only kind of life to really live, and you gave that to me after so many years of needing it."

He took her hand and led her back to the table. It took him longer to sit, and they both knew why and smiled over the situation, so thankful for it.

Before their second round of drinks arrived, their perfect evening was interrupted. Approaching their table mouth-first was an old family friend of the Donohues', Cassie Morgan, eying Jason suspiciously as she spoke in her fake, upper-crust accent. Everyone knew Cassie was from Detroit's Lower East Side; no upper-crust accents going on there.

Amber acted glad to see her, but it was actually a drag being pulled from desire and into doom. Cassie had been known to spy dirt on perfectly clean people. Amber could hear her mother mentioning her and Jason at a secluded little table in a sultry nightclub, compliments of the mouth of the century. What she did and who with was no one's business but hers, but it would be common knowledge now. The family would be as giddy as junior prom queens at the very idea of Amber being out with another man. Nothing was sacred in her family. They were masters of making mountains out of molehills.

As usual, Amber was her usual pleasant self, but acting surprised over the ghetto Joan Rivers was a pure acting job that she'd no doubt get an Academy Award for.

"Cassie, how nice to see you."

"Darling, you too. It's been ages."

Amber felt a little sickened. *It was two damn months ago at my nephew Eric's graduation party.*

However, Amber was not the true hot spot. For some reason, Cassie couldn't take her suspicious eyes from Jason, and it wasn't due to his looks. No, something scandalous was cooking; Amber saw it and tried to steer the situation. "This is Jason DeMaras. I might be selling my jewelry in his store."

She reached out a hand. "Really? How nice. I always knew Amber's jewels would sell . . . eventually. I don't have any of my own but—"

Jason stood, taking the already outstretched hand. "Amber makes the best I've seen anywhere, and I'd be glad to show-case them. By the way, nice to meet you."

Amber loved the way he got to the point with the mouth of Detroit and the surrounding suburbs, putting her in her place before she said something really stupid.

All Cassie could do was regroup, pathetically. "Yes, she is good. I should know, I've been everywhere, seen everything, including good jewelry; just getting back from Paris, you know."

Well la-dee-fucking-dah, was what Amber's mind was saying, but her mouth remained polite. "Jason is the assistant manager at Roma Shoes."

Eyes stared big time. "No wonder your name and face are so familiar to me. You probably sold me my last pair of shoes. I'm always in there."

"I can't place the face, but I do see a lot of women, Ms. . . .?"

"Morgan, and that's perfectly fine, darling; there is a lot of traffic in Roma." Her eyes rolled back to Amber. "I must be going; Damon awaits. Just wanted to say hello, having not expected to see you here, Amber Marie. Tell the family hello for me."

What for? Surely, you'll see them before me as you spread news of my appearance with Mr. Fine as Wine. And who bet-

ter to do it? You work faster than the six o'clock news. "I'll make sure to tell everyone. See you soon." *Only if hell should freeze over!*

Jason said his good-byes, then turned to Amber. "Is she always that gauche?"

"She's a pain in the ass, literally speaking."

That evening, Jason took her back to her car, which was still parked near the entrance of Lilly Ruben, but took her hand before she exited. "One more kiss good night?"

Without a verbal response, she moved into his arms, kissing the corner of his mouth in tiny nibbles before planting a wet, juicy kiss across his lips that he'd never forget. Their mission was so undercover and secretive that she could feel the seat of her lacy panties get wet all over again. His plundering fingers certainly didn't help the situation as he slid slowly in and out of her in strong, even strokes. She never wanted to leave his arms or the inside of his car, fearing she'd never regain quite the same magic they'd discovered. But with Jason, each time they were together was an entirely different world of sexual desire. The only thing that scared her: love was quickly following; the id was certainly on overdrive, but along for the ride was a heavy dose of superego, the very thing that forced reality back into a world of unbridled passion. She slowly pulled away, fearing the love aspect was still a one-way street.

"I have to go, Jason. You know what happens in the morning—work, work, work."

"Right, getting everything prepared for your opening."

"There's always a lot to do for one of those things."

"I know, but can't you leave from my house in the morning?"

Though she wanted to be there, she also didn't want to wear out her welcome mat, something she feared had happened to her and Maurice. Jason was different, special, and she wanted him to stay that way. Mystery always keeps a fire hot, words her mother constantly repeated, and for once, the advice was correct. "I have so much still to do tonight. I have to make sure the crimp pliers are sharpened, the bead cord in supply, the—"

"I get it. Another time then?"

The disappointed look on his face saddened her. Her gentle fingers caressed his cheek. "I'm sorry. I just don't want to wear out my welcome with you."

"You could never do that, Amber. I know you have a life, and I'm just thankful for the time we've shared." He shut off his ignition. "I can walk you to your car, can't I?"

He walked her to the car, waited for her to disarm it, and watched as she slid into the seat. "You go right home, Amber. Wouldn't want anything to happen to you. Hell, I just got you, and I want to hang on for possibly another one hundred years."

"I'll call you when I get in, tell you I'm okay."

"Good."

Before her door was closed she said, "Wait! I have something for you." She reached into her purse and handed him a tiny satin bag. "I almost forgot these."

"What are they?"

"Crystal studs. I wanted to give you something special."

"You've done that already just by being with me, but what made you think to give me these?"

"There's a tiny crack in the one on your left ear."

"I never noticed."

"I did."

He kissed her briefly on the lips. "You notice everything, don't you?"

"Only when it matters, and it does with you."

"Get going before I make you stay the night with me, Ms. Wonderful."

Amber watched Jason drive off, already missing him, already counting the minutes before she'd be in his arms again.

5

all falls down

Jason hadn't called or come by in weeks. Amber was on the verge of thinking her antics in the car had been a complete turn off for him. After all, he was still a man; and she'd refused him after giving it up to him so soon. She could feel her ego and superego laughing at her in the background, saying: *See, I told you so. Why must you be so willful and give in to that damn pesky id?*

Before truly wallowing in self-pity, she realized she could have easily called him again. She'd called his cellphone and left messages at the store, but to no avail. And as tender-hearted as she was, she took it for rejection. Moving too fast. That damn id, the troublemaker of the century.

However, with her grand opening less than a week away, she didn't have time to sit and mellow drama-side over the antics of a man who may or may not have felt put out. She didn't feel in her heart that Jason was that kind of man, though. Something was up, and it apparently had to be worked out on his side. The only thing left for her to do was pull up her big-girl panties and move on.

Just when she was getting her mind out of the toilet, she saw her mother approaching with a big bucket of Kentucky Fried Chicken. *God no! I already feel like shit! The last thing I need is Mom helping me to stay that way.* Reluctantly, she unlocked the shop door and smiled. "Mom, this is a surprise."

All pleasantries were immediately cut short by her mother's curt words. "You and I need to talk, Ms. Thang!"

What the hell? "Talk? About what? And why am I suddenly 'Ms. Thang' again? I haven't been that since seventh grade when you caught me in the garage making out with Jeffrey Cooper."

"And I'm basically here for the same reason." She pulled out a chair at Amber's small dining room table and ordered, "Bring over some paper towels and sit."

"Christ!"

"Don't sass me, Amber Marie. Just do it."

Mechanically, she moved to her small countertop to retrieve foam plates instead but continued her so-called, sassy words. "Tell me what this is about. I'm thirty-two, Mom. You can't just come in here and treat me like I'm twelve years old."

"I can when it comes to my own child doing the unthinkable."

"The unthinkable?" Amber plopped into a chair across from her mother. "Get to the point with this, Mom. You're sounding most unwell, if I may quote a line from *Titanic*." That seemed fitting since she felt she was drowning in bullshit, anyway.

Her mother stared at her in disbelief, then lowered the bomb: "I saw Cassie Morgan the other day."

Here we go! The mouth of the metro area has struck again. "And this means exactly what to me? Seeing Cassie isn't a big deal. We see her every Fourth of July, Memorial Day, Thanksgiving, Labor Day, and any other day she chooses to come by and spread terrible news. Hell, we even see her on Halloween— fitting since she's a witch, anyway. What makes seeing her special all of a sudden?"

"Two words, Amber: Jason DeMaras."

"What about him?"

"Cassie saw you two together in some nightclub. He's that cute shoe salesman you've been drooling over for damn near two months now. Yes, I know of your window-shopping escapades with him, and all the rest."

"And?"

"And he's married, Amber."

"What? Mom, Jason isn't married. He's divorced."

"And you believe him?"

"I believe him as much as you and the rest of the family believe every word that comes from Cassie's cesspool of a mouth!"

"Don't be arrogant. Cassie's niece's best friend's sister is his wife, Gina."

"Really took a steep climb on the family tree for that one, didn't you?"

"The fact, Amber, is that I don't want you hurt."

"Jason isn't going to hurt me, and he's not married." *Then where is he?*

"I think he is. He looks like a playboy, and Cassie hasn't been wrong to this day. She's the one who discovered Frank and Julie having an affair right behind your sister's back. You remember how hurt Yvonne was about that, don't you?"

Suddenly, the once tasty-looking chicken on her plate now looked like a giant glob of Kentucky Fried grease. She pushed the plate aside. "Suddenly I'm not so hungry. What's your point?"

"The point is that I've been watching you the past few weeks. You've been in the dumps, and I think it's over him."

"True, I have been upset about not seeing him, but it's not because he's married. Now, if you don't mind, I have a garnet necklace to finish for my window. You do know my opening is Saturday."

"I know what's going on with you, believe me. I knew it before you were born. You kicked harder than your sisters, and you're still doing it. Leave him alone, Amber, he's trouble."

"Mom, please! I'm not a kid. If he's married, which he isn't, I'll deal with it alone. Come on, I've got work."

"Fine, I'll leave but don't expect me to be sympathetic when you find out something you don't want to hear." She politely wiped the grease from her perfect, too-red lips and tossed her plate of bones into the trash. "I'll be home in case you need me to cry on."

Amber stopped her mother at the door. "Do me one favor. Stop listening to Cassie. She doesn't know what she's talking about. She's like a black Hitler; all she has to do is salute and everyone goes crazy."

After her mother drove off in that fancy yellow Benz convertible that her father slaved to buy, the emotions hit again, making her second-guess her situation. *Does Cassie have a point this time? Why has he not called me? Jason! Where are you? Where are you when I need you?* For the first time, she found out how terribly controlling and wicked the id really was.

Unable to rid Jason completely from her mind, she walked over to the sofa where they'd made love, still smelling his aroma on it. What an intoxicating aroma it was, so manly, heavenly, his true essence. She missed him.

The grease from her few bites of chicken, coupled with her mother's talk about Cassie, made her nauseous. There was still a little time before she set up her window display, so she lay across the leather sofa, remembering what she did to Jason, how his masculinity felt between her lips as she sucked and seduced him into a ravaging, erupting volcano. Reliving how his juices felt against her fingertips made her smile for the first time that day. The way his taut, bare muscles felt against her palms as he rocked up and down on her made the world go away and her hands descend to the aching V between her thighs; aching from need and want, something that only Jason could completely and methodically alleviate.

It was like he was actually there, staring down at her with a smile sexy enough to melt her butter. The way his eyes scanned her slowly, as though he were savoring her for the ultimate feast. That was the thing about Jason. He had such a way about him that he could make a woman come just by winking at her. The day he winked at her in Roma Shoes, she felt that burning twitch—the kind that drilled upward, vibrating everything in the vicinity. She had come so close to losing it just by one of his glances. The night that he stared glassy-eyed at her dripping wet sex, she knew there'd be nothing greater in life than having him inside of her, any part of him, every inch of him.

Visualizing his snake of a tongue coiling, sliding, and wrapping itself around all her pleasure spots made her back arch off the sofa. He'd done it again, made a thin film of silky perspiration cover her skin surface. Her fingers immediately moved to the source of the potency, unzipped her jeans and quickly moved her panties aside. It was slick and hot inside, and it became volcanic the minute her fingers massaged an already-sensitized clit. Her mind went on journey after journey, imagining Jason touching her, kissing her in every exposed spot, remembering how he sucked every ounce of her liquid as though he were drowning and liking the idea of it.

He had bent her body in so many positions that she nearly fell from the bed one night. Now was the same. Her fingers were now his, and she dug for gold. Minutes into her fabulous fantasy, her body shook, her eyes squeezed shut, and she could hear herself screaming his name out at the top of her lungs. It was mad, wild, crazy, but when reality really sank in, what she did to herself could never be as exciting as it was with Jason. Her body reacted nonetheless, quivering in quick, tight waves, spreading her legs so wide apart that a million Jasons could move in right for the kill.

When the pleasurable torture subsided, her eyes opened wide. Perspiration covered her body, wetting her silk blouse, making it stick to nipples so high, tight, and raw that they hurt. They hurt like that the other night until Jason's lather soothed them; lather from his lips and his orgasms. He spewed like no other man ever has that she knew of. He was beautiful, more beautiful than ever before as he poured himself mercilessly onto her chest and stomach. That was the aroma that lingered, and though she was now very aware of where she was and what she'd just done, she loved the scent in the air. It was him.

Once the heavy breathing stopped and she returned to Troy, Michigan, she realized she'd let herself go way too far with him, and apparently now it was time to pay. Was he hovering above Lake Michigan laughing and having a grand time with Maurice at her expense? That she didn't know, but there was one thing she knew for sure—the store opened on Saturday, and she had to be ready, Jason or not.

Saturday morning.

The storefront looked incredible; painters had managed to get her colors right, blush and bashful, though to her mother, the colors were pink and pink. Amber knew that was what lack of an imagination did to people. They saw reality and nothing more, never letting their mind fly to other worlds. Hell, it took her and her sisters almost ten years to get Mrs. Donohue out of Michigan for a day trip to Chicago. Of course, there was no imagination going on there, either.

Loads of hot pink, powder pink, and sky-blue balloons filled the outside of the store and drifted down the short block. What made everything perfect was the sun. It shone so brightly that by nine that morning it looked like midday, highlighting window displays that even Amber had to slap herself on the back for. The multitudes of gemstones fixed and fashioned in intricate jewelry designs made the windows look spectacular; something a true jewelry lover would fly into a shopping frenzy over.

The designs were all made, and the store was gorgeous. Invitations and flyers had been mailed out, and the caterers brought in platters of breads, seafood and other cold cuts.

She was set. It helped to stay busy or that infamous id would have taken her back to that sofa for another tour down Jason Lane. No happs! Amber knew she had to ditch any thoughts of him because he, apparently, was only after one item; that thing. The thing that makes men try to crawl back into the womb every chance they get. Maybe for the first time in the history of the world, Cassie was right. Maybe Jason was married and decided his little taste of temptation had been enough.

The opening was a success, style reporters from Channel 4 and Channel 7 covered the highly anticipated affair, due to Amber getting to radio and television publicity people almost two months in advance. All of her family made it, even her mother and the flighty Cassie Morgan. Hell, with her there, who needed the news team? One thing Cassie did that really threw Amber for a loop was buy the second most expensive piece of jewelry in the store—a black and white, diamond-studded crystal necklace. Cassie was actually nice and helpful that day. Either she got the news that Jason was history and wanted to help in the emotional recovery mission, or she pretended to be nice so Amber could give her a reduced rate on jewelry. Either way, Amber was glad to have additional cushion from her mouth.

The entire time, Mrs. Donohue walked around the store gloating to whomever the fuck would listen, while toting a martini. *Yes, this is my daughter's venture; my very own daughter! Imagine that!* Didn't she just sound too much like Sophia in *The Color Purple* mouthing off in the juke joint?

Mrs. Donohue spent the rest of the time trying to convince Amber that she was right about Jason. To Amber, that wasn't helping the situation. What would have helped was if Cassie hadn't mentioned Jason at all to the family. The news spread like wildfire, and different people came up to console her about the situation as though someone died or something. There was no relationship, just active daydreams that needed to be relived over and over again of what they did on her sofa and bed. Amber's only thought was, *This is not a funeral, guys. Back off and buy something. Drink some punch.*

By the end of the day, Amber was tired, and the place was littered with wilted balloons, meat trays left half-eaten, drink cups all over the place, but, most importantly, money in her cash register. Yes, Exotica Jewels was a hit. This was the first time she would actually have to have stacks of her business cards reprinted. Everything turned out great with only one drawback: no Jason; not even so much as a congratulations telegram or call. She shrugged her shoulders, talking to herself in a listless voice, "Life goes on—somehow."

6

---

i heard a voice this morning

The moon never looked as gorgeous as it did the night she stayed late at the store. She'd stepped outside to take a breather from looking down at screw eyes and needle-nose pliers, things she used to make women beautiful with her designs. Though she was busy and making cash beyond cash, Jason was still on her mind. Another month of no calls, no anything. She rebounded as well as possible, pulling up yet another pair of big-girl panties and getting on with life.

Her gaze returned to that big, beautiful moon with stars cascading around it and could feel something in the air. She couldn't put a finger on it, but it made her feel good, free. Maybe that feeling meant independence from her family, a sudden slew of major income, and, yes, getting over a man who wasn't destined for her. The media coverage, word of mouth, and flyers made Amber Marie and her fancy jewels the talk of the town. People were coming in, placing orders, and finding hidden jewels like never before. They were selling like hotcakes; husbands buying for wives, wives for husbands, sisters for mothers. With her finances being the way they were for the last three weeks, she knew she'd be able to afford that two-year-old BMW-Z5 she'd had her eyes on over at European Motors if sales continued.

Again, she gazed upon the moon and stars and knew something was going to change. She could feel it! Amber walked back into the store, finished a back-ordered set of malachite and onyx earrings, then closed shop feeling good, really good for the first time in weeks.

She heard a voice the following morning, heard her name called in the distance, but since it was so early, she attributed it to being sleepy. Once inside, she slid the cover from her bubbling latte, sipped it, letting the sweet aroma bring her to her senses, then got to work in the back parlor on customer orders.

The chimes on her front door jingled and Amber looked at her watch. *Is it time to open already?* It was only nine-thirty, and she didn't open until ten. *Why the hell didn't I lock the door behind me?* She quickly investigated, walking into the parlor slowly with a pair of wire cutters in her hand. There the intruder was. The cutters dropped to the floor, but her feet picked up pace, approaching him. "Jason?"

He quickly turned around sporting a dashing smile that soon left after seeing her not-so-happy expression. He held his hands up in defense. "I know you're mad at me, baby, and you should be."

"Where have you been? I've called your cell, gone by the store. Nothing! Nothing from you in over a month, Jason."

"I know, and I'm really sorry. Things came up, and—"

"Things? Life happens, Jason, but that doesn't mean you forget your friends or someone who should be just a little more than a friend."

He walked closer, holding his hand to her. "Can I at least explain?"

"Explain what? You missed the opening and everything. Everyone was there—the news, my family, friends, my—"

"Amber!"

"What?"

"Your family is one of the main reasons I wasn't here. I know that sounds lame, but I need to tell you why." He handed her a manila envelope. "I need to give you this first. It just came back from headquarters."

She eyed it skeptically. "What is it?"

"Open it. You'll like what's inside."

Amber slowly took it, sat at a corner table and proceeded to open the package.

Jason moved closer, staring down at the loveliest woman he'd ever seen, and she looked so good in her navy-blue pantsuit with contrasting white piping. He hated having missed the past month with her, but taking care of business was imperative. Now that business was together, he hoped he could still be in her life.

Amber just stared at Jason. A half-smile covered her face as she fingered the edges of the document. "Is this real?"

"Definitely. I'm sorry it took so long, but they really like your designs, Amber, and I wanted to tell you in person. How soon can you get some things together for Roma?"

"Like immediately. I can't believe this."

"Believe it. The contract is real. All you have to do is sign it. Need a pen?" He removed a ballpoint from under his suit jacket and handed it to her.

Watching her sign something that would totally make her happy made his day. What would make it even better was to feel her skin on his, taste her lips once more, climb into her sugar, and drench himself within her—that would make what he'd gone through lately so worth it.

He hadn't heard her call his name until she practically screamed it out. "Sorry, I was wrapped up in watching your excitement about the contract."

"No, you weren't. What were you really thinking?"

"Forget what I was thinking. How do you feel about selling more jewelry?"

"Excited. Hardly able to believe it. I'm almost a chain."

"What do you mean?"

"If I had another store, I'd be a chain and a half."

"Then you'd be too busy for me."

"I think you're the busy one, Jason. I haven't seen you in weeks; then you tell me my family is the reason you haven't been around." She handed him the signed contract. "What's up with accusing my family? I know they're not the greatest people on the face of the earth, but you can't blame them for you not being around."

"I'd love to explain if you'd give me a second!"

That took her aback, not quite expecting him to respond that way. She shrugged her shoulders. "Fine, explain. Start with the married part first. Yes, Cassie told me you're married."

"I thought you didn't listen to her."

"After you disappeared, I had no choice but to believe her."

"I'm not married, Amber. I told you Gina and I were divorced and that we'd tried getting back together for the sake of my two-year-old. But it didn't work." He slouched into a chair, reluctant to tell the rest, but knowing he had to. "Amber, what I didn't tell you is that Gina and I were still together but not married, just living together."

It felt as though all the blood in her body was draining from her body. "What? You're still with her? Oh my God! I slept with you and you still belong to her?"

He pulled her arm, making her face him. "Amber, the word is *was*. True, when I met you I was still with her, but it was rocky. We weren't sleeping together, just sharing a house and arguing all the time. When I saw you, well, I kind of went crazy. I wanted you so badly that I could hardly breathe."

"That's not a good enough answer."

She tried jerking away, but he held on for dear life. "Amber, wait a minute. The reason I didn't contact you was because I felt bad about sleeping around on her, but after thinking about it, I knew she and I didn't have a relationship, anyway. That's when I decided I had to make the split. I didn't contact you because I was working on things, moving completely out of her life so I could be with you. The only way I wanted to see you was if I was totally free—free to be the man you need me to be in your life. I know my tactics were crazy but I didn't think you'd understand. Please believe me."

"So what Cassie saw wasn't true?"

"She knows someone who knows Gina. I didn't want the news to get out and back to Gina. She's got a terrible temper, and I wouldn't want you hurt. Honey, I'm free from her. I was getting out of it, anyway, but you gave me the push I needed." He pulled her closer to him, standing. Their faces barely inches apart. His voice lowered an octave, almost overcome by needing to kiss her. "Amber, when I made love to you, that sealed it. No other woman could do it for me. You're the only woman I've pursued like this. Don't let a stupid mistake on my part break us down. I didn't know what to do when that lady was staring at me. I knew she knew me."

"Shut up, Jason."

"Amber, please."

"Shut up! I can't hear this right now." *What the hell am I doing? He has apologized, and you know you love him. Give it up, girl! Once again, id, one point, Amber, a fat zero.*

"Amber, just listen to me, please, baby?"

"Just shut up, Jason. Shut up and kiss me before I go ballistic."

"Really?"

"I said shut up."

He'd always been good at following orders, and from that point on, her orders were the only ones he heard. Tasting her again was like waking up to a new life; she felt so good in his arms, tasted like the richest chocolate—soft, smooth, creamy—and he couldn't get enough of her. The only thing on his mind was finding that famous blue leather sofa and christening it again.

The more he moved into her, the more her body molded to his, allowing him entrance to any part of her he wished to explore. His tongue nipped at her neck, swirling over her delicate skin, he smelled her perfumed hair and tangled his fidgety fingers around her short bob. "Amber, you didn't get rid of that sofa, did you?"

"It's still here, but I open in a few minutes."

"You're open now; wide open for me, baby." His hands slid across her derrière, feeling its tightness. He wanted to dip inside, make her languid, free and hot to him. "I love you, baby, and I've missed you so much. I hardly say those words to anyone. My parents and my children hear it all the time. Now I want you to."

"I love you, too, and I think you know that. I don't say those words very frequently, either."

"Then let me show you our love is real, just for a minute." He slid her crepe shell up her back and grazed his nails delicately across her skin. He loved how she wiggled to his touch, giving a quaint little chuckle, yet not stopping him.

The hooks on her bra finally snapped loose, and her id reared its pleasure-seeking head, gaining momentum. Her lips were saying no to him, but her body pressed against his as though she were already naked within his clutch. "Jason, we shouldn't. Someone could see us."

"Then let them watch. Who knows, we could give them such a good show that they'd be willing to walk out of here with one of those expensive gemstone necklaces of yours. You'd be full of money and full of red-hot meat sliding in and out of you."

"You're a mess."

"No, I'm just weak to you, princess. Give me a little; then I'll leave. I swear."

"Take what you want, because as you already know, you're not the only one who's weak."

"If you give me an inch, I'll take a mile, and you know that, girl. Let me lock the door."

Each second away from him was too long, and a lifetime wasn't long enough. The moment he made contact with her again, she was ready for him. His hands moved up and down her sides, exposing her hardened nipples. He quickly latched on, sucking from one to the other, wetting, licking, tasting them as she secretly screamed out with pleasure.

His lips traveled south, crossing her stomach, kissing it every inch of the way, then lowering the elastic waist pants to her hip joints. All he could do was stare in wonder at what was behind the lacy navy-blue panties and wonder how much she'd let him have of it.

What he didn't know was that the sky was the limit as far as she was concerned. She'd given in to the willfulness of that insane id long ago. Now she was simply going with the flow. Her tender voice quivered out, "Take it! Take it, Jason, and diminish it!"

"Indeed!" He pulled slowly on the garment until curls of feathery brown hair met him. He toyed with it, gently fingered it until everything was exposed. He kissed the strands, letting them tickle his lips and chin. The scent of sex saturated her skin, making him wilder and hotter for want of her thick nectar—waiting to watch as it spilled from her.

He kissed her soaking, feverish folds, then stared up at her. "You want more, baby?"

"I want anything I can get from you."

He parted her thighs, licked his tongue quickly across her folds, then inserted two fingers. With smooth, even strokes, he rocked those two busy fingers so deeply into her, fascinated by his own actions. The more she moaned with intense pleasure, the more he watched, excited by how deeply his fingers could disappear inside of her. The pace was steady, manipulating her G-spot until it hummed like a perfectly oiled machine. That's what he liked; that was the second point to his venture. The first point was satisfying a queen.

Amber cried out to his pounding rhythm and closed her eyes. Her nipples were so hard that they swelled. She lifted the shell and squeezed her aching breasts as he looked on in utter amazement. Her hands were full of plump, tingly breasts, squeezing them, making the buds harder and harder until she could barely stand it. Coupled with the pressure of what he was doing below, she totally lost it.

Amber losing it meant one thing to Jason; a handful of perfumed cream, the essence of her femininity. The more she delivered to him, the stiffer his erection got, pressing hard against his pants. "Amber, you're making me so hard, so thirsty for you."

"How thirsty?"

"Thirsty enough to drink every ounce of liquid you have."

Her body vibrated against his fingers, pounding, over and over until finally the roar was down to a whimper. Her liquid covered his fingers, and he was so ready to taste them in slow, lavish licks.

When he stood, he placed her hands against a shaft desperately thick and hard. His rugged voice was barely able to form words. "I need that release, baby."

Amber quickly unzipped his pants, reached for his snake, massaged it hard, up and down, palming him, squeezing it, jerking it, rubbing his tip and scrotum until he erupted into a sea of milky white. She wanted to collapse again at the sight of it, but needed to get every inch out of him, satisfy him, claim him.

His lips met hers again and again until they decided they'd gone way past their few minutes of eroticism. A wet, warm cloth in her private bathroom made him as clean as a whistle again. At the door, he kissed her, then slowly pulled away. "I've got something for you but didn't bring it in case you didn't want me in your life again."

"Yeah, like that could happen. You know how weak I am for you."

"You gave me a good scare, though. I really thought you were going to throw me out."

"I'm not that stupid. What's the surprise?"

"I can't tell you. Meet me for dinner and I'll bring it."

"I'll cook dinner for you tonight. Say about seven?"

"I can't wait, girl."

7

---

crab legs and chianti

When you own your own business, you can close up shop whenever the mood hits. Amber was all too glad to do that for the ultimate date. She hadn't seen Jason for so long, and she wanted everything to be perfect, from the food to the blush and bashful polish on her toes—pink and pink, in other words. Her mother stole the phrase from *Steel Magnolias*, but nothing about that evening was going to include her mother. She had done enough damage by listening to Detroit's mouth of the century—Cassie Morgan. No, tonight belonged to her and Jason.

Before getting home, she picked up a package of crab legs and a bottle of Chianti for a meal prepared for a king, her king. People came from miles around for Amber's grilled crab legs, and the butter—God, the butter! Melted down to perfection and seasoned with lemon juice, garlic and onion powder with a pinch of Cajun seasoning. Amber knew if the meal couldn't trap his ass, nothing would. However, that was her least concern. From her kiss alone, he was hooked like a giant swordfish.

As the crab legs cooked to tenderness, Amber showered in her favorite shower gel, Pheromone, savoring it and letting it drench her body in all the perfect places, all the places she hoped Jason would conquer again, starting south, working his way north, with a lingering visit midway! Yes, the thought of Jason touching any part of her body sent her on a physical journey that had bypassed any trip previously taken. That included anything Maurice tried doing to her—poorly.

The messy crab legs would ruin a dress, so she decided on a tight pair of jeans and a clingy T-shirt with the silhouette of a black cat stretched across the breasts. The damn thing would meow like crazy after being stretched by her voluptuous breasts. After she put the shirt on, she stood before the mirror, smiling at how it stood out against perky bosoms. "Yeah, he'll love this since he's a breast man, anyway!"

By seven, everything was done. There was a nice Caesar salad awaiting him, buttered rolls, and of course, the crab legs. For dessert, her. If that was too presumptuous, there was always the key lime pie she bought. Looked good as hell, but she knew she tasted better than a store-bought pie. After fixing the table with her best silverware and china, with the crab basket in the middle, she lit a Blue Nile incense in the living room, ready for a perfect evening with a perfect man.

Seven-fifteen on the dot, Jason's Cadillac bounced into her driveway. She was rocking to the sounds of Unwrapped's "Tupac Tribute Medley"—a total jam to get up and boogie to, but she decided to stay on the sofa and let him ring the bell two times. After all, she didn't want to seem too anxious, despite the fact that all she wanted to do was swing the door open and jump him. Not sophisticated enough.

On the second ring, she was on it! When she opened the door, she was nice and calm, smiling at the sight of him and relieved that he'd actually showed up. "Jason, you're just in time. The crab legs and rolls are almost done."

He stepped inside, toting a bottle of wine and something else in a pretty, lavender bag. "Crab legs? Really? I love those things. Good thing I dressed for the occasion. Seems you're dressed for it, too."

She smoothed her hands across the tight-fitting top, making damn sure her breasts were accentuated. "These old things. I just threw them on so as not to ruin a dress."

His eyes slowly scanned her super-shapely form. "You look good, girl; good enough to eat. Forget the crab legs. And I've got just the thing for that top."

"Really? What?"

Amber watched him walk across the room sporting his own pair of tight jeans and a grass-green polo, one that showed hints of muscles everywhere on him. He was strong, lean, and stacked, everything she liked in a man, everything that made her drool. She knew by the end of the evening she'd need a bib. So would he, if she had things her way.

Before that evening, the only thing she'd seen him in were dress slacks, nice business shirts, and, oh yes, his own flesh. Yum! However, his casual appearance was something she could definitely get used to.

He sat down on the sofa, spread his thighs apart, and patted them. "Come on, sugar. Let me give you what that kitty shirt needs."

Amber proceeded to sit next to him, but in one movement, he hoisted her into his lap. Their faces were so close together that she could see tiny, dark brown freckles on his face, something she hadn't seen before, something that made him sexier—always something more to discover on him. A thin film of sweat formed above his stripe of a moustache, which she proceeded to kiss.

"Hold on, Amber. Let me give you what you need to really set you off." He pulled an orchid corsage from the lavender bag. "All beautiful women need flowers. I thought about a rose, but that's too typical. You need something exotic."

"I love orchids."

"You are an orchid, and I'd love to smell you every day." Jason grabbed the hem of her shirt and pulled it over her head, tossing the garment to the chair across the room.

"Jason, what are you doing?"

"Putting the flower where it needs to be." He pinned the flower to her bra strap, then squeezed both breasts together, staring down at the plump mounds with wide eyes. "Girl, my nose is so wide open for you that I can smell chicken frying in a kitchen somewhere in lower Ohio."

Giggling at his response, she said, "Where in hell do you come up with this stuff?"

"It's easy when I'm around you. I damn near went crazy those weeks not being with you."

"Can't have that, can we?"

Their lips met in passionate waves of desire, nibbling, sucking, gently pulling. His tongue circled hers, dipping into corners that missed him so much. His hands moved up and down the softness of her back and sides, toying with her bra, wanting to snap it apart but not wanting to spoil her excellent evening by moving too fast. Judging from the aromas coming from her kitchen, he knew she'd gone out of her way to cook something grand for him. Had he taken that bra apart, dinner wouldn't have mattered to him anymore. He'd have been too willing and ready to eat her in luscious tongue strokes all over her body. The idea of touching her pristine body in such erotic ways almost made him let go, saturating his pants to the max. With her, he couldn't help it. Just hearing her name made his body react in ways no other woman had ever inspired. For the time being, he settled for a sensational kiss, drawing from her well of desire as much as possible while his hips rocked to her rhythm.

Amber could feel the power in his kiss and in his hip movements. He drained her every time his thick, wild erection pressed against her fragile, soaking-wet core. She briefly thought back on the first time she saw him, having not seen a man that pretty before. She was stunned, awe struck, but knew someone like him could never be in her life. No one as fine as Jason ever gave her the time of day, other than that sickening Maurice. That was then. Now the unthinkable was in her arms and delighting her senses with every kind of excitement imaginable.

She continued to move against him, rock to his flow, and kiss him in ways she'd only seen done in erotic movies. The heat and friction were so powerful that she took his hand, placed it against her throbbing crotch, and let him rock her.

For Jason, that wasn't enough. He had to feel the *real* heat, stoke the *real* fire. He slid her zipper down, quickly found that throbbing G-spot, and massacred it. It hummed proudly for him before exploding. He bucked a little, enticing her with words he only used with Amber. "Do it, girl; drip all over me." He felt her tension release, squeezing his fingers within her pleasure spot. He looked into her flushed face in amazement, his voice soft and withered. "What do you do to me, girl?"

"Everything you want me to."

He fingered the now-crushed orchid. "I'm afraid I crushed your flower."

"Let's set it in a plate of water. I wanna keep it forever, as a token of you."

"A token of my love for you."

Jason saw the immaculate kitchen with a perfectly set table. "I've got a good idea."

Amber turned in time to see him stretch the polo over his head, showcasing pecs and ripples to slaughter for. "Why are you taking your clothes off?"

"My idea, have a picnic in the middle of your bed. We can spread a blanket over the bed, sit in the middle of it, and get just as wet and greasy as possible. For dessert—massage in the oil and have a funky good time. Sound good?"

"Only if you pour the Chianti."

He grabbed the Chianti, a shitload of crab legs, and followed her into the bedroom.

Sitting in the middle of the bed on a blanket with crab legs and wine never felt so appetizing. She did that all the time, but being almost naked and sitting across from a bare-chested Jason took everything to a new level. As promised, they got as greasy, sticky, and juicy as they could.

In the background, *The Lover* was playing on Amber's

VCR, left over from the night before when she fell asleep to it. Watching it now would completely set the mood, help hot love scenes of their own to come to fruition. Jason started the game after dinner, smearing more of the leftover butter sauce across Amber's nipples and aggressively sucking it off.

She giggled at his advances. "Don't you want to watch the movie?"

"I want to do exactly what they're doing, but more, so much more, Amber. Get what I'm saying?"

Amber seductively smeared the runny butter across her warm flesh, feeling it trickle across her body, drain down, and saturate all the right areas. She patted the pillow next to her. "I get it, baby. Better yet, I'd like to *get it*, and in just the way they're doing it."

Both briefly looked at the TV screen, seeing the actors making love in an art form so poetic, so artistic that Amber and Jason were enticed to go beyond, way beyond anything any Hollywood cameras could capture. And doing it their way was the only way to get things done in her bedroom.

As Amber laid back to accept him, he climbed aboard, straddling her, forcing her to stare up at the massive bulge pressing against his zipper. Nervous excitement warmed her hands as she pressed against a clothed rod seemingly the length of her arm, wanting only to peel off his pants.

Jason was no help. His words beckoned her, encouraging her. "Slide it down, baby, and take it." He massaged her buttery breasts, taking them into his hands, rolling his thumb across the hardened buds, loving the sight of her back arching to him. The more he massaged her breasts, the more she rubbed his crotch, creating friction, heat against her palms. He stiffened within her grasp, allowing the feel of intense pressure aching to be set free. She felt his form, the tip of an erection so ready to plow through her that it felt rock hard.

That's what she wanted, and that's what she got. Hurried fingers slid the burning zipper down, inching closer to desire that was only a slice of material away. Her anticipation for him was so great that she could barely breathe. She exposed his taut thighs, sliding his jeans to his knees. Unexpected words escaped: "I want more, Jason."

"Then take it." He lifted the band of his Jockeys, reached inside, and stroked himself, squinting his eyes to the idea of those fingers being hers. He replaced his hands with hers as they both slid his underwear down.

Outstretched to her was a phallus so hard for her that it was pumping, moving on its own from desire. God, he was so beautiful, every part of him, from his hair to the purplish tip of an erection that could, did, split her in two. The feel of him in her hands tightened her core, doubling the intensity of her arousal. Her whisper-soft voice called to him. "Now, Jason. Now. I need it. I need it hard, hot, and raw, every single inch."

"You do, indeed, but you need it my way." With her hands still wrapped around his throbbing shaft, he reached for the rest of the butter and handed her the tiny dish. "Drip it on, slowly. Cover every inch and suck me the way you did those crab legs. Girl, you sucked that meat out *so* good that I almost came from the sight of it."

"Was it that good for you?"

"Not as good as what I want now. Pour it on and annihilate me."

The first drop of butter gave him a buzz and he wanted to let loose on the still-warm butter, but needed to give his Amber something real. Yes, she was definitely his, wanting to explore wild and exotic venues the way he never thought to with another female. Amber took his mind on a journey south of the border, and his body straight to Erotic City!

The butter dripped across his shaft as Amber, with haste, rubbed it in, paying attention to every vein and ripple before working her way back to a demanding tip. Her slippery, butter-soaked fingers played in his center, forcing moisture from it, wanting to taste his nectar once again. Her excitement rose, making her body writhe for him, making already hot nipples feverish.

Jason's feather touch across her cheek barely took her attention. "You want it, baby, don't you? Talk to me."

"I can't talk, Jason, just give it to me."

"Take what you need; suck me dry and drain me, girl."

He leaned forward above her, bracing his hands on either side of her head and positioned a super-fine, juicy ten-incher at her lips. The buttered tip played at her lips, and he smiled at her enjoyment. "Claim what's yours."

Amber wanted him so badly that her cheeks caved in from each stroke; taking him in, sliding all of him against and down her throat. Looking up and seeing his hips thrusting against her was but another dream come true. The man she knew she loved was loving her back, not hovering above some lake sporting a diamond. He was really there with her, and she took full advantage until she literally felt like bursting from need of another type of satisfaction. Those pleading, needing words briefly forced her lips away from him. "Now, Jason. *Now!*"

At her very command, he pulled back, stood from the bed to rid his jeans and hers. With longing, lust, and love in his eyes, he mounted his angel, kissed her soft lips once again, then slowly fed inches upon inches into an open, dripping well. Thighs soon wrapped high around his body, giving him the warmest, most incredible feeling he'd ever had. Suddenly, nothing was more important in life than taking Amber to new heights. And with that in mind, he rocked her, pumped and pulsated so deeply within her that he felt crazy. Yet, he continued, staring down into a face so pristine and perfect that sex alone couldn't have accounted for it. She was naturally beautiful.

Amber's screams set him off. Feeling her hands all over his body, including his scrotum, made him pump harder. Hearing his name being called with his primal, thunderous thrusts destroyed his sanity, and he delivered, over and over, rocking her steadily until both were too exhausted to know their own names.

Jason collapsed on top of her.

For Amber, the heavens opened then. Jason *belonged* there with her, in the intimacy of her bedroom. Her home was really a home, now.

Late the following morning, Amber rolled over to an empty pillow. She could smell him, smell their lovemaking in the air, but where was he? In the past, her first instinct was to assume their good thing was now gone. But there was something in Jason's eyes last night that told her he was hers, for real and forever . . . yeah, right. She told herself not to be so romantic—then saw a folded piece of paper sitting on top of the television. Amber quickly opened it, reading the brief note. *Meet me at two. 1306 Lafayette . I've got the ultimate surprise for you. I love you, baby.* Signed, *your man.*

Yeah, like he hadn't already given her the ultimate surprise weeks ago and again last night. Lafayette, though? What was down there other than the downtown district? A special lunch maybe? For the next hour, the only thing that occupied her mind was seeing Jason again, not his surprise for her, not anything except seeing him.

8

isn't it just grand—again

Amber arrived a little after two and saw Jason standing near a building looking at his watch. She presumed he was counting the minutes until her arrival, hoping he was. She couldn't wait to hop out of her car and run into his arms.

As she approached him, she noticed how impeccable he looked in his navy pinstripe suit with silver shirt underneath; incredible, but not as incredible as he had looked in the raw only hours ago. She snuck up behind him, taking his hand into hers. "So, what's this big surprise my man has for me?"

Before he even spoke, he took her into his arms, landing the most passionate, loving kiss on her that he'd ever given to anyone. Breathless inches apart, he smiled into her sunny face. "I know this will be hard to believe from a man like me, but I have really fallen for you, Amber. I know we've only known one another for a little while, but I have urges for you that go way beyond our sexual relationship."

"Why would that be hard to believe from a 'man like you,' as you say?"

"I'm a little rough around the edges, barely out of one relationship before getting into another. I have a daughter from one relationship and a son from another. I'm not the boy next door, Amber. I've been around the block."

She mussed his hair. "And with that voyage around the block, you still managed to come out looking and smelling like a rose. I'm not in love with your relationships, Jason. I fell for you and everything you are. No man is perfect, but you come pretty damn close." She nuzzled closer to him. "Now, what's this surprise? A lavish lunch, a shopping trip for more shoes?"

"Even better than that."

Amber watched him fish inside his pocket, wondering if an engagement ring was in there and not hovering around the world's bodies of water with Maurice. Accepting an engagement ring from someone she just met over a month ago normally wouldn't have been her style, but in Jason's case, she'd make the transition.

He pulled a slip of paper from his pocket and handed it to her. "After you read this, look at the building behind you."

Her questioning eyes searched his. "What? What do you mean?" *No ring?*

"Just read the paper. It'll explain everything."

After unfolding the paper, she silently read its contents. *Owner, Amber Marie Donohue. Two hundred square foot property located at 1306 Lafayette Blvd. Renovation underway by At Work Construction Co, Est, 1980.* Her hands shook, a smile curved her perfect pink lips. "Jason, what have you done?"

"It's yours, baby. You're a chain."

Amber just stared at the building, then shouted, "I'm a chain!"

"You're that and more. Everyone in jewelry in Detroit is talking up a storm about Exotica Jewels. No kidding, every piece in our store is almost gone. You know that; I gave you the back orders."

Ignoring his words, she kept on gleefully. "You bought this place for me?"

"I bought half, and I'm financing the rest."

"With my help."

"No way. This one's on me. I missed your other opening, and I'm really sorry. I made the purchase over those weeks I was away from you." He looked at the building, then back to her. "Do you like it?"

"I love it. I love you." She moved into his arms in the middle of a crowded avenue and kissed him, not ever wanting to leave his arms again.

Two months later.

More Exotica Jewels had its opening on a bright sunny Saturday, and it seemed the world was there. Included within that world of people was Cassie, making her usual smug comments. "Who'd have thought my best friend's baby sister would be a chain?"

"I'm not little anymore, but I definitely am a chain, thanks to my man."

"Are you the reason he made that break from Gina?"

Instead of answering, Amber poured Cassie another glass of punch. "Spike it, please! The gin is behind the bar."

Meeting her at the door was another unwelcome surprise—Maurice. He strutted in with a chick on his arm. Amber could hardly believe her eyes as the tall, good-looking half-Asian Maurice took her hand. "I knew that necklace Ava bought had to be your design. It's distinctively Amber. Love your shop."

"Why . . . uh . . . Thank you?" She hadn't expected Maurice to be so kind.

"Don't be surprised by the compliment. I always thought you were smart, one way or another."

"Smart enough to leave high and dry?"

Maurice looked at the fussy-looking, toothy-grinning blonde on his arm. "Excuse me a minute, Ava. You know how it is with old girlfriends. They can't stay away from me. Besides, Amber and I have some catching up to do."

"Old girlfriend! Who the heck—"

"I didn't mean it to sound that way, not really; although you are a few years older than I am."

"This conversation is over, Maurice."

He pulled her hand. "Come on, just take a walk with me to the other room, get to know one another again."

Not that she really wanted to talk to Maurice in a secluded corner and get to know him again since there was nothing to know. She cut to the chase. "What do you really want, Maurice?"

"To congratulate you on your success."

"You could have done that in front of Buffy, Bambi, Barbie, whoever!"

"It's Ava. Don't be rude."

"You're right; she seems sweet, but don't embarrass me, Maurice, especially at my own opening."

"You're still my girl, Amber. You'll always be mine, and don't forget that."

That appalled her, making her stare at him as if he had acquired a third eye and a lot of money-grubbing hands. Her finger and head action got in gear; then she remembered where she was and who really was her man. She took a deep breath, stared Maurice in the face, and politely unloaded. "You sure didn't act like I was 'your girl.' Besides, aren't I a little old for you? And, if I may quote Erykah Badu, who gave you permission to *try* and rearrange me? Certainly not me! I have a man, Maurice, a real man; one who won't leave me stranded and take an engagement ring that *I* purchased. Look at him, Maurice; he's perfect, and when I get a ring from him, he won't be hovering above Lake Michigan with it."

"What?"

She gave him a smug grin. "If you have to ask, it's not worth explaining. Go and buy Toothy-Fruity a pair of my earrings. They may do something for her, and you!"

Jason met her halfway across the floor, peering in Maurice's direction. "Who's that?"

"A blockhead from my past."

"Are you okay?"

"Other than the fact that my mother, Maurice, and Cassie are here aggravating me, I'm fabulous."

"Yes, ma'am, you are. And since you're so fabulous, follow me into the storage room."

"No way! There's too many people here for that, Jason."

"Just one kiss."

"Okay, but that's all you get until I close."

The minute the door closed, Jason's lips attacked hers in a powerful, explosive and tremendously wet kiss. "Are you having a good time, girl?"

"It just got better."

"Good, because in a few weeks, I'll have another surprise for you."

"Another store?"

"Not quite."

"Give me a clue?"

"Fine, you want a clue?" He stared briefly to the ceiling, thinking, then back down at her. "What is it that slides on pretty, delicate fingers and looks stunning when the light hits it?"

"A diamond?"

"Maybe. What is it that hovered over Lake Michigan with Maurice?"

She smiled and caressed his cheek. "A diamond ring?"

"You guessed it! Don't worry about me hovering over the lake with it. I hate the water—too many mosquitoes."

"I'll supply all the bites you'll ever need."

"That's my plan, girl."

They kissed once more before rejoining the crowd.

lovin' it

Have you ever seen a man who was so gorgeous that he should have the words *I can fuck the living daylights out of you* stamped across his forehead? If you have, that would be Orlando, my husband. No man anywhere was that fine . . . I thought!

The alarm went off, and Orlando clumsily hit it in a sleepy stupor, stopping the aggravating noise before it awakened me. Too late. I rolled over and stared at the flaming red numbers—5:00 A.M. "Damn, baby! Why are you getting up so early?"

The love of my fucking life rolled on top of me, casting his wicked smile against the streaks of hot Florence sun already on the horizon. "Today's my first day at work for Water-Vision. It's not every day an engineer from Boulder gets the chance to help build new waterways in a place like this, baby. I just want to keep celebrating."

"But five in the morning?

"Sure. Why not?"

"You don't have to be in until nine."

"Exactly my planning, sweet cheeks, and I mean that literally."

I smiled and caressed his soft brown skin. "I guess you do mean that. You squeezed them enough last night."

"A butt as juicy as yours, girl, a guy can't help himself.

That's why I set the clock; I didn't get enough last night. I think that damn champagne got the best of me."

"But you'll admit the pre-anniversary festivities were on jam."

"Right on." He rolled over on his back and pulled me along. "You ready for me, baby?"

"I'm a constant inferno and always willing to be melted down." I smiled into his already blushing face. "Do it."

"Your wish is my command, Mrs. Candy."

He lifted me onto a rod so hot and thick that I thought it was the middle of the night again. One that hard and high was usually too worn-out the next morning to rise and shine. Not his, the rise was *so there* and the shine was all mine.

The minute his tip met my already wet flesh, my world shook, my body trembled, and I let him slide so deeply into me that I could feel him in my thoughts. There was only one set of thoughts on a one-track mind—how my baby could jam.

First his rhythm was slow, sliding with friction in and out, teasing me as he gripped my hips and made me suffer in slow motion. He spread his legs farther apart, sliding in a little deeper. By that time, smoke seemingly came from my ears and eyes, and I could barely stand the pressure. I kissed his wonderfully hungry lips, nibbling first his bottom lip, then his top. The more he pressed into me, the more eager my tongue became, tasting hints of last night's champagne, until his rhythm beckoned for deeper pleasure.

I rose up, stroking such wonderful pecs that ached to be rubbed, palmed, and teased. The thing about my husband, his body was so smooth and soft, yet hard in all the right places, and I loved the hell out of touching any part of him. My fingernails grazed his nipples, leaving streaks of love across them. The feel of his erect nipples against my hands made me pound harder against him, grind him like metal against metal. I had to taste him, feel those hard pecs against my tongue and lick him in quick laps. My tongue against his sweaty flesh did it for him; his back arched, and his eyes now more exposed to the sun, quickly squinted shut. His incredible lips murmured the most erotic words, making me want more of what he was already doing, meshing deeper and deeper into me.

I was so full of him that I nearly felt like exploding, shattering bits and parts of my body across the room. The cops would have found my DNA all over the apartment had I let go the way I really wanted to. With Orlando, I had to take it slow, rock him until he sprayed. A man like him came in such erotic ways, his love potion flowing into me, filling me, boiling hot! I took my time and inched farther south, methodically, expeditiously. He had awakened my wrath at five in the morning and now he had to suffer the consequences.

I slid from him, feeling so hot and hollow without his flesh pumping inside me, but it would be worth the temporary separation. He begged me not to leave him hanging, but my tongue had a mind of its own as it trailed the length of his chest and stomach. He soon clammed up and let me work my damn magic. My tongue traced the definition of his well-proportioned six-pack, darting into every single crease, then licking down to his navel. His muscles tightened, and he spoke as best he could during the delightful torture. "What the hell kind of a tongue do you have, girl?"

"One that can set the world on fire, but I'll start with you."

"Damn straight you will."

The game was a good one to be played, and I played it well, making him my personal Strip Monopoly board, allowing him to drive his hot, slick convertible right into my hotel . . . the hotel of desire. When my tongue licked his tip, I thought he'd lose it, but he remained as calm as possible; what a good boy he was.

Devilish tongue swirls against that skyscraper of an erection almost took me to the limits, but he needed my total attention, and I couldn't help but focus. I licked in upward strokes, like he was a rocket ice-cream cone with creamy filling. I devoured him over and over, seeing his face tensing, knowing his end was near . . . so was mine. A knot continuously coiled tighter and tighter inside of me, winding me until I thought I'd pop! And I did; he could see it on my face as well, felt my slick skin, and he asked, "Are you doing it?"

I couldn't talk, just shook my head, and in one swift move, he pulled me back on top and squeezed everything into me. One quick jam and he could feel my muscles tightening around him, squeezing him like an anaconda. He reached back, grabbed the side of the headboard, and rocked. We banged so hard that we knocked a hole in the wall, but I didn't care. I wanted mine and that's all that mattered to me.

The rush came again and my body constricted around him so wildly that I thought I'd kill him. I did, and he loved it. Still, I wasn't done. I'm never done until the volcano erupts. I got everything I could get because my baby poured into me, squeezed every thick, creamy drop into me, and I gladly drained him.

We rested in complete euphoria for moments before one of us had the strength to speak. "Happy anniversary, girl."

I smiled into his dreamy eyes. "That was the best gift yet."

"Wait till' later. You'll be steam-pressed."

"Can't wait. It'll be a long day until you return to me."

He kissed my forehead. "I'd better get into that shower, girl. I could stay in this bed with you all day."

"Why don't you?"

"Baby, it's my first day. I can't call in sick. Don't you want daddy to make you a lot of money?"

I made my own money, always had, but that sweet question deserved an answer. "I could live off your love."

"Sure, for two days max, then that stomach of yours would start growling. Can't have that." He kissed my stomach in circles, beginning to get excited all over again. "Hmmm, maybe I can stay a little longer."

I looked over at the clock, nearly six-thirty. Knowing he had to make it across town and try to find his way in a new country, I nudged him, realizing he was right in the first place about getting out of bed to start his day. "There'll be plenty of this for you tonight."

He slowly slid from the bed, casting his shadow against the walls. Goodness, my baby was so well hung, making me hungry again as I daydreamed of him mixing with me, and he'd just left my body. There was something about him that I simply couldn't get enough of. Maybe it was the *way* he loved me—deep, sincere, totally in love with me, as much as I was with him.

Orlando was something new and refreshing to me. He inspired me to be my best in everything I did, from loving him to loving myself. That was so unlike what I had in Boulder. I'd wasted too much time listening to my family badger me, rehashing my past and I'd had enough of it. When I met Orlando, I knew he was the one for me; no more men who were already involved with other women. The stress of eight solid years getting my DDS made attached men look like the solution. Just sex, no commitments. But that quick fix had cost me.

Getting the hell out of Boulder with him and a wedding band on my hand was the best thing I could have done. I was no longer the family's example of who not to be like. I was now the married one, doing it right and making it last. That actually killed my sisters and cousins, that I was proving them wrong and actually making a good life for myself. The fact that I was starting my career in a fabulous foreign country added to my self-confidence. By the end of the month, Candy Buchanan would be the new dentist in an established practice in Florence. An expatriate friend had helped me with all the red tape. For people who hate bureaucracy, Italians sure do have a lot of it.

Between sleeping around with men who didn't belong to me, I managed to get an education. See, there's more to me than a slamming body. The really good part is Orlando respects both aspects of me. He saw my potential the day he brought his cousin into my office on Columbia Street in Boulder. I fixed Tyler's cavity and got a date for myself with the very attractive man who brought him in. It's been smooth sailing ever since.

I watched Orlando slide his robe on and tie a knot in front. That bulging erection parted it, making me lucid again. With hunger still in my voice, I said to him, "I sure wish you could come back to bed and spend another hour playing around."

"I need to shower, get you off my skin."

That perplexed me. He never wanted my aroma anywhere else than on him. I had to ask. "Get my scent off you? Why?"

He leaned over, kissed my forehead. "Because, darling, if I walked into work smelling of you, every man in the vicinity would bust his ass to get to you. You'd have to use that wicked little drill to defend yourself."

I laughed. "You really feel that way about me?"

"Baby, I love you. You're so good to me, damn!—how you look. Even at six in the morning, you look like a sex kitten. Every time I sex you down, you get prettier. How do you manage that?" He kissed me again. "Now, let your king take his shower and set off to make you a bunch of money."

"Can I shower with you?"

"That won't help my cause, Candy girl. The reason for the shower is to smell like a man, not like sugar . . . and your sugar would be all over me, like now." He tightened his robe, then left me in the middle of the bed to think over what we just did. I don't know, there was something about that man that could make me implode, willingly, morning, noon, or night, 24-7. I lucked out with him, and because of that, there was a constant smile on my dark brown, considered pretty face.

Once I heard the shower and him splashing around in there, I laid back and imagined exactly what he was sudsing up in there. The thought of his sponge soaping the length of his massive rod killed me; the idea of gentle sprays of warm water trickling down on it, making it harder and harder, stiff as iron, made my thighs open again. The idea of being in that shower with him made me fantasize.

Within minutes, I was screaming out his name, but he couldn't hear me and rescue me, so I rescued myself, straight into the Climax of the Month Club. I was so into it that I hadn't heard the shower shut off or him fishing for a dress shirt in the other closet. When my eyes finally opened, there my beautiful husband was staring at me with the most enticing smile on his face. The enormous tenting in his sexy suit pants totally put me away, though the right words always found a way out. "Come on and get in the bed with me. What else can you do with that thick, dark snake in your pants?"

"Pray that it'll slither away and let me work the rest of the day. Don't stop on my account, though. I could see everything straight up to a heart I know pumps only for me." He checked his watch; mouth now dry, words hardly able to come forth. "Save some of that for me tonight. I swear I'll make the wait well worth it."

"I know you will, baby. You want breakfast before starting your day?"

He winked at me. "I already ate, and it was mouthwatering. Girl, how you cook!"

I wasn't exactly the domestic type. But in Italy the food was so fantastic, it was actually fun. I almost wanted to cook dinner every night after doing root canals. Almost!

"You'll need something more to sustain you before you eat that lunch I packed for you last night."

"Yes, Dr. Buchanan. Whatever you say. How about eggs and pancakes?"

"You have time for it?"

"I'll make the time, baby." His eyes had a look of euphoria.

"What's on your mind, Orlando, other than sex?"

"Just smiling at how miraculous you are."

"What do you mean?"

"You managed to make an incredible dinner last night, make love to me and still have the time to pack my lunch."

"Of course. How many husbands do you think I have that I'd do anything for?"

He took me into his arms and kissed me with hot, burning lips. "I really lucked out, didn't I? Good thing my sister was in the hospital having their second child and couldn't take Tyler for his dental appointment. I'd have never met the love of my life, would I?"

"I'd have found you, Orlando. You were meant for me one way or another."

He planted one more kiss on my lips before releasing me. "What did you pack?"

"Something you would look forward to—garlic bread and spaghetti carbonara."

"I didn't smell that cooking yesterday."

"I made it while you were out and put it away before you could eat it. Besides, if you recall, I had something else planned for dinner last night."

"Indeed." He tapped my behind. "Let's eat that breakfast. I'm suddenly so hungry. I think it's that workout you gave me forty-five minutes ago."

He sat across from me eating a stack of pancakes and pouring gobs of syrup over them. I couldn't help but smile. "Orlando, you must want cavities on every tooth. Besides that, you're going to get sick from all that syrup."

"I like sweet, sticky things. That's why I married you." He poured a little more on while I watched and listened to him. "So, what's planned for you today? You're not going to stay around here when a beautiful city awaits you, are you?"

"No, I plan to get out, and see a few things; maybe a few museums, do some shopping. I hear they have really good meats at the market square."

"That's a bit of a trip."

"I have the time. Besides, I want tonight to be extra special for you. I'll buy the meat, marinate it, and make it nice and juicy for you."

"I'll do the marinating, girl—on you tonight when I come home."

"That's sweet, but you'll need sustenance before you get royally laid."

"True, so what else do you have planned other than buying meat and museum hopping?"

"Lunch with Denise if she can make it."

"Wish I could come along."

"You'd get bored listening to Denise and me over lunch. Since she moved here three years ago, all she's done, other than work at the embassy, is proceed to screw every Italian man who's willing to spring for dinner and a show."

"She gets away with it."

"She is gorgeous, but she reminds me a little of myself before I met you. As you know, I did the same thing."

"You were just killing time before meeting me."

"It was a little more than that, and you know it."

Orlando shook his head. "Is that why that expression is in your eyes?"

"What expression?"

"You look sad. I saw it early this morning after you awakened. I thought making love with me would have taken that away. What's really on your mind, Candy? I know it's got something to do with your family, this day of the month, and this anniversary. Spill the beans."

"I'm okay, really."

"Candy, I've known you for over five years. By now I know when something is wrong with my wife."

"It's just that their expectations of me haven't changed."

"How do you know that? You haven't actually spoken to them in months."

"Right, months. They didn't even come over to say goodbye to us before we left for another country. Another country, Orlando!"

"I know that hurt you, and it apparently still does. What have I told you before? Fuck them! They're not worth the effort of stressing over."

"They're my family. They could have called to see how we're doing."

"The day is still young, Candy."

"I know, but they won't call. They never have wished me a happy anniversary."

"That's what this is really about, isn't it? You're still trying to prove something to them even though you're Dr. Buchanan now. You don't have to prove a damn thing to anyone but me, Candy. Even at that, you have nothing to prove." He took my hand into his, kissing it, rubbing it across his cheek. "Baby, what really matters is that you have been a dream come true to me. Remember, you saved me as well. Before you, my love life was nothing but one meaningless encounter after the next, wondering if this or that one was the one, but no one was it for me, Candy. I wanted a wife."

"My escapades were for the hell of it, Orlando. I wasn't looking for commitment, just a good lay. Wild, crazy medical students who've been deprived for too long sometimes fall into that trap."

He devoured the last of his drippy pancakes, swallowed his coffee, then smiled at me. "That life is over now. You have me anytime you need me. Hell, I'd lay you every day if you'd let me."

"And I'd be a widow before the age of thirty-five. I'd wear you out."

He stood, taking my hand. "I'd be glad to oblige, but don't worry, I'll be around for a long time, Candy girl." He looked at his watch. "I'd better go and find my way around. Do something fun today; have a ball with Denise, and don't worry about your family. They're the ones who need to wise up, you already did by walking down the aisle with me five years ago." He kissed me once again—a long, drawn-out, lush kiss. "A little something to keep you warm and toasty for me, baby. Cook me something good, now." He winked, playing the role of traditional husband to the max. "I need strength to fulfill your favorite fantasy."

"And what would that be?" Delivering a devious smile.

"I think you know the answer to that!"

I watched my baby throw a leg over his new Vespa and pull away from the parking complex. After the front door closed, I leaned against it, thanking God for sending me such a magnificent husband, and just in time before I went stone nuts.

I sat at my dining room table to plan my day. The first thing on my list was getting my darling husband off my mind long enough to think. I needed wine, flowers, salad fixings, and meat . . . there I go again, because the only *meat* I was thinking about was Orlando's. No, what I needed was fine Italian meat for the most scrumptious veal parmigiana I've ever made. The market square would definitely be the place; Denise told me it was the best place for good meat. At that, I showered.

It was a particularly hot day, the kind of hot that's hazy, humid, and bright before 10:00 A.M.; the kind of hot that makes you sweat like crazy and want to pull off everything and walk naked through the streets of beautiful Florence, Italy. Who would care? People are free here and are always ready to admire a lovely work of art. Even I must admit that I have a body to kill for—long, lean, and tanned, everything an Italian man would look to the heavens and give thanks for. However, getting arrested wasn't my thing, and I wasn't daring enough to go nude, so instead I put on my crepe red-and-white polka-dotted sundress that hugged every curve, dipped into a vicious V, and stopped at midthigh—downright scandalous. The matching red open-toed stilettos added more mystique. The thinness of the dress's material was airy enough to keep me cool—for a minute!

I checked the mirror once more before leaving just to make

sure I was as fly as ever. I'm the kind of woman who has to look damn good before I go anywhere, whether it's to the store or the trash can, doesn't matter. I'll take a compliment from anyone, anywhere. That's just me, and it works like a charm. Orlando already told me that I'm beautiful. Husbands are *supposed* to give those compliments, but it never hurts to hear it again and again from strangers. When I hear it from my baby, however, it's all good!

My first stop was to pick up a beautiful bouquet of fresh flowers and prosecco from the local shops to have on the table that night; next I would have a quick little luncheon, then be on my way to the square. Needless to say, I got side-tracked before I'd finished shopping. There's a lot of things in Italy to grab a girl's attention—and I eventually met up with the ultimate distraction . . .

It was only 11:00 A.M. by the time I'd purchased the wine, so I was able to take it home, refrigerate it, then go back out to enjoy more of the sights. There were throngs of people in the marketplace. Festive music filled the air, and everything was stunning, like something out of a picture postcard. I was truly glad my husband's job transferred him here. Everything was so beautiful, fresh, fragrant, delighting my senses almost as much as Orlando had several hours before. The many varieties of flowers for sale made everything around look like an Impressionist painting—vivid and eye-catching. How could anyone not notice such beauty? That would be like walking past a field of purple and not seeing it; that's the Alice Walker in me.

I wondered if my own husband was out somewhere enjoying the sights instead of getting to work early. Who could blame him? From the looks of the crowds on the streets, I seriously doubted that anyone did anything but shop around, buy liquor, and chill out the rest of the day. Who could blame them? The day was hot and sunny, a good day to be out and to be with a lover. Too bad for me since my lover was off making lots of money. Then something hit me—a little thing called *control*. I was so into Orlando that the slightest things made me think of him. I'd come a long way from that silly young woman who just wanted a lover, any lover; didn't matter to me back then.

I hadn't seen the right bouquet on the streets, so I ducked into Vinucci's Milleflore to buy the perfect flowers for my husband. Carlo Vinucci himself helped me arrange the perfect mix of flowers I know back home as Red Rocket carnations and Wild Romance asters—the perfect mix to get Orlando's *red rocket* in full gear, as if he needed help! And if I had things my way that night, those Red Rocket carnations would live up to their name, shooting my wicked imagination straight to the stars. I picked them up and handed them to Signor Vinucci. "Definitely wrap these up." Even after a crash course in Italian, I still spoke English.

The elderly gentleman, the epitome of Italian courtesy, smiled at me and did his share of flirting. "*Si, si*. A romantic evening planned?"

"My husband and I are celebrating two monumental occasions—our fifth anniversary."

"Many congratulations. And the other?" the eager Mr. Vinucci questioned.

"We're living in the city of pure, unadulterated romance, and I plan to make the most of it. We moved here from Colorado, a nice place, but I like Florence better. I love the romantic flair of Italy."

"Indeed, a lovely woman should 'ave the romance as much as possible." He patted my hand. "And you—*bella, bella.* What a lucky husband you have."

"I think so. So does he."

"Just to talk to you does an old man good. And it helps to practice the English for me. Maybe I get lucky, too."

"Oh, Signor Vinucci. Just wait for the next hottie to come in and steal your heart. She'll be around."

He wrapped the flowers and placed the wonderful bunch in my arms. I was good to go. I still had shopping to do, so I asked him if he could refrigerate them for another hour while I finished my shopping. He was only too glad to have another opportunity for me to grace his store. I promised him that I would return in an hour. With a kind smile on his face, he placed them in back and waved good-bye to me. "Ciao!"

I stepped back into the midmorning sun, and that's when it happened. The minute I walked onto Vinucci's flower-laden patio, I saw something so outrageously sexy that I thought I'd dissolve into the flower garden. A sexy-ass hunk of a man walked by me in pleated beige linen dress pants, creamy yellow shirt and tie. I hadn't gotten a really good look at his face, but judging from his side profile, he was out of this fucking world!

His wavy black hair was shining so brightly in the sun that it looked blue-black. His olive-brown skin was smooth and beautiful, something I hadn't seen much of in Italy. Sure, there were dark people here, but this man was not Italian; he was beautiful and black—and American, like me. My eyes narrowed, and I followed his scent; bet your damn ass I did.

Before I even knew what I was doing, I was trailing behind him. I mean I fixated on him like nothing else existed in the world. That's what got my panties in a twist and made me think about my actions. I hated myself suddenly for even wanting to look at another man when I had the best husband in the world that a woman could possibly ask for. My man was hot, beautiful, and made almost as much money as I did. What else could I possibly want?

The man in front of me.

Apparently, it took only one look to sway me, and I was hooked like a fish on a line. With my strong attraction to the male sex, I wondered if my family was indeed correct about me. Did I really want something different after only five years of marriage? Or was this just a game?

After all those years, I was suddenly swayed by the first juicy man who strutted by me. I *was* weak. But I followed, like there was a magnetic strip across my damn forehead, drawing me closer and closer to whoever the hell this man was. I accepted my fate, acknowledged that maybe I was fated to have multiple lovers, and skipped happily along. A fool for love—or maybe just a fool.

Getting next to him, this total stranger—was a definite plan of action.

I watched how he moved, how his arms swayed as he walked, everything the man did made my nipples hard. Instinctively, I wanted to touch each hardened bud, wishing his hands were squeezing and manipulating them; sucking them . . .

I got weak in the knees over the thought. I hadn't planned on letting him know I was behind him, but the very idea of his lips on my now moist skin was making me lose my grip on reality. He turned and glanced at me, but not before I saw how sexy his ass was. My husband was but a mere memory, sorry to say. I could just imagine this man's thin mustache tickling my vulva, nipping and sucking on my clit, my slick feminine folds, all the while driving me into the most intense orgasm I could ever imagine having. I almost lost my footing when he smiled at me as I had that damn daydream. His eyes were so lovely, almond-shaped and dark brown. I wondered just what else on him was dark brown. From the looks of him, he was probably a good, healthy nine inches.

He kept walking, and I kept following. All I wanted him to do was jump into my game and play me all night long. I could imagine him sliding his fingers deep into me as well. Imagine, all that juicy rod and three of his large fingers inside of me, pleasuring me, teasing me, spreading me apart. I was so near the verge of coming again that I could feel my nectar bubbling inside of me. This stranger was tongue-dipping fabulous.

The thing about it was that, at that point, I didn't even care that I was married; I was too involved with the vision of his tongue mating with mine. How I could just see his lips covering mine, going deep into me, then moving down to each nipple, gently raking his teeth across them. The honey really started dripping, hot, thick, and wet against my core when I imagined feeling his deliciously long tongue entering my wetness, dipping deeper and deeper, dodging in and out, swirling around inside of me until the very essence of me drenched his lips and chin.

I had to squint to keep the sweat from dripping inside of my eyes, because he was making me hotter than fire. After my vision cleared, I realized I'd been after him for six blocks. I was quite sure he knew that I was following him like a child follows the Good Humor truck. He was better than ice cream; he was a walking porno flick.

I hadn't a care in the world where he was going. For all I knew, he could have taken me on a guided tour of hell and back, and my flames simply would have burned deeper, stoking me, scorching everything in sight—just the way I like it. He wasn't taking me to hell; I was already there and enjoying the scenery. Wherever he was going, I was sure to be right behind him, watching his walk, his sway, everything associated with smoldering hot sex . . . wearing tight beige pants.

What surprised me was when he entered the Bargello National Museum. How the hell could he have possibly known the museum was on my list of places to visit? Was this man, this complete stranger, reading my mind? Whatever the case, I'm sure to him it was a good read, because he turned slightly to me, smiled, making sure I was right there with him, then entered the museum. Like the puppy dog I'd turned into, I traipsed in right at his heels.

The Bargello was magnificent, just the way friends described it and just the way the postcard depicted it. As beautiful as it was, it was still overshadowed by the man leading me on a guided tour of complete and utter satisfaction. He stopped at the internal courtyard. And me? Well, I stayed a little behind so as not to be too super obvious. Hell, I had to have a little mystery about me, didn't I? Damn straight I did, but it wasn't working with him. He expected me, drew me inside with the carnal knowledge of a sensual chase underway.

What a grand pursuit it would be.

He was right. Within seconds, I was there. I had to be, because there was now a hunger in my soul, primal, lustful, and nothing but setting my eyes on him could satisfy my desire. Maybe I was man-hungry, insatiable, and all those other *cute* words that fit my predicament, but I managed to keep it real, staying just enough behind him to make the chase more enticing. The more wild and wicked a situation is, the more uncontrollable the human mind is. I knew that was the case for me; with him, I only hoped.

He looked out at the botanical gardens, yet, from the corner of his eye, he watched me slowly approach, moving in closer and closer, as though I were a casual spectator. He knew the game, but for me, it wasn't quite wicked enough, so I played him—well.

I approached the railing of the garden, looking into a place that looked like it could have been the actual Garden of Eden . . . and there Adam was standing so close to me. The only thing wrong with the picture was that Adam's fig leaf was so not there! How he could have teased me, making that leaf rise, revealing inches upon inches of full, pulsating length, just like the proverbial snake, waiting to entice me into forbidden pleasures.

Despite the fact that my thighs were wet, sliding against each other causing the most intolerable heated friction a body could endure, I moved in closer; so close that I could smell him. I don't know what he was wearing, but he had on enough of it. His aroma was a natural husky cologne and man-mixed. He was making me high with his scent alone. I leaned in for more of it, but he walked off, leaving me hanging, hungering for more.

A story up was one of the main attractions and something I was dying to see—other than Mr. Hot and Spicy—the room of Donatello. I knew something about the great Italian sculptor. I'd minored in art as an undergrad. I figured that would be my angle with that beautiful gentleman; get in close enough to start a conversation, make him realize that I was smart about something and not just a woman following the most sensual man ever created around Florence, Italy, hoping for a really good screw. Was I not her, though? I was, and I was fitting into my role with such ease, though there was still something in the darkness of my mind that knew what I was doing was wrong—wrong to my Orlando.

The minute Mr. Fine-as-Silk walked into the room, he made sure my bouncing thigh-high dress was fluttering behind him. When I walked in, he casually turned his head to the statue of David, my personal favorite for all the right reasons—nudity, grace, depth, and a body to liquefy for.

I knew my perfect stranger under his clothing was beyond what any statue possessed. He looked great in his clothes, however, but what an awesome power he had to be in the raw. My God, the idea of moving my tongue up and down his rippled six-pack sent chills up and down my spine; imagining how his stomach would heave in and out while my lips did their thing on the band of his Hanes. The idea of sliding my hand inside of those briefs and grabbing a cock as thick as my wrist was controlling me. You know you have it bad when the mere thought of a man's body sends you into overdrive and spiraling down the highway to explicit nirvana. He was doing that to me, and I was but a willing participant.

Par for the course, I made my move, standing side by side with him while staring at a naked statue. Again, his aroma intoxicated me, drew me closer to him, and landed me merely inches from pleasure. We quickly glanced at each other, both too nervous to say anything, to get any real action going, but the drama was so thick and intense that we were barely seconds from getting buck wild and crazy in there on the marble floor. The other gallery-goers seemed not to be there or maybe it was because we just didn't care anymore.

I could tell he was a little on the nervous side. He'd rub his hands together, look at the sculpture, then briefly at me. His nerves moved him from David, to Hercules, and finally to King Neptune. All nude, all sticking out to the stars and back, like he was. The sight of his clothed erection lit my fire, and I moved to him again, making him sweat like crazy.

That's what I wanted, and I was damn sure going to get it. He wasn't going to start anything, so I had to. I moved in on him as he stared at King Neptune, who had everything hanging out, spears in each hand, and looking like a major testosterone spill. Knowing that I was looking at engorged male anatomy only got my stranger harder. He had to have it, and so did I, so I cleared my throat. "How long have you been interested in Donatello?"

His beautiful dark eyes met mine, taking me whole, melting my heart. *Please, don't let him smile at me.* His delectably thick lips and thin mustache smiled into the most orgasmic smile imaginable. My legs went weak, and the only thing holding me up was not wanting to look crazy in front of the very man I wanted to fuck!

"Quite a while. How about you?"

Christ! That voice, that wonderful, body-drenching, mouth-watering voice! Was it possible for a man to sound better than he looked? The day proved that anything was surely possible. I had to steady myself. "I know a lot about him but seeing the actual work just blows my mind. I studied Renaissance art in college for my minor."

"Really? Someone as lovely as you could have been a model for one of these Italian geniuses." His eyes slowly scanned me from my long dark hair to the revealing dress I was sporting. I loved how he looked at me. I wanted him to do so much more than look—touch, yes, touch, all day, all night, baby.

He continued, "What do you know about him?"

Could I speak without sounding like a gibbering fool? I had to try because first impressions lasted a lifetime, as would my memory of him if I could just have him for ten minutes.

The professional in me arose with such charm and knowledge that I actually surprised myself. "I know that Donatello was born here in Florence in 1386; he never married, had no children and got his start in the shop of the very ingenious Lorenzo Ghiberti. Donatello created the shallow-relief technique."

"And that would be?"

"Oh, that's a way of making a sculpture seem deep but actually carved on a shallow plane."

"You are a smart one, aren't you? I love smart women." A hint of tongue poked out, gently wetting such succulent lips, kissable lips, lips to suck and kiss all night long.

That kicked it into gear for me and I smiled. "I don't know about the smart part, but I love art. This David was one of the first free-standing nude statues of the Renaissance era."

His brow raised seductively. "I can see you like looking at him." His wonderful deep eyes moved to the hem of my dress, scanning my thighs briefly before remembering who he was. I knew who *he* was— someone so hot, rich-smelling, and smooth that I was minutes from meltdown.

Before I could really move in for the kill, he smiled, gave me a nod, then headed for the Michelangelo room. I kept my distance, watching him walk the exhibits, stopping briefly at the *Apollo, Ebbro,* the *Brutus,* everything naked and taking it all in much the same way I was. Only with me, a naked Apollo wasn't doing it. The more I stared at him watching nudity, the more I imagined it was him on one of those sculptor's turning platforms . . . and I was the sculptor, molding him to perfection with my hot hands, eagerly caressing an already engorged phallus.

The idea of all that packing dark meat sliding inside of me almost gave me an orgasm. By the time the quaking in my body ceased, I was almost directly behind him, a light film of perspiration covering my forehead, my hands jittery and ready to reach for him, pull him into me and taste his tongue in circular motions. Slow, sweet, and severe! That's what this total

stranger was turning me into, something wanton and feverish, getting close to him again was the only cure.

He was studying the wealth of sculpture, the differences in
Classical and Renaissance styles, and I approached again,
standing next to him, saying nothing, barely breathing. For
seconds neither of us knew what to say or how to say it without giving away how we really felt and what we really
wanted to do. Somehow he saw me scanning him, looking at
his long, slender fingers, wondering how deep he could go.
Would he know what to touch and how to touch it? Then I
looked at him and saw the man I knew he truly was. As badly
as I wanted to experience him, I held off.

The entire time he had this odd smile on his face, one that
a statue couldn't be responsible for. No, that expression was
from the scent of a woman. His fingers and hands calmed, relaxing to me, wanting me to experience more with him than
just the pleasure of appreciating great art. What I knew he
wanted was an overflowing dose of true nakedness, but not
on a pedestal. Not still and hard to the touch. He wanted me
and I knew it.

I thought again of Orlando, which brought me to the ques-
tion of why I was in a museum with a perfect stranger—and
I do mean perfect. What I had was called the can't-help-its.
But I was scared. Not of him. Of myself.

Just when I'd decided to go on about my business as though
I'd never laid eyes on him, he spoke again. Funny how one
thing can trigger you into doing all the wrong things no matter how much you want to be right with the world. For me,
that was this man's voice again.

"Which David do you prefer: Michelangelo's or Donatello's?"

"I like them both. Donatello's is more human, but Michelangelo's is heroic."

"Which physical qualities suit you more?"

Yours. "Having both in one package is always enticing. A

woman rarely gets that. It's either one or the other. Your preference?"

"I couldn't say. However, being everything to a woman is always a good idea, never a practical and attainable one, though."

His expression softened, and I looked down at his wedding band. He was also married. Two of us walking wide-eyed into a pit of lust and at someone else's expense, unfortunately. I felt bad for a minute, but this man had to be experienced. By me. In a big incredible bed, wearing nothing but a hard-on. He excited me more than any man I'd ever had. He was intellectual, interested in me, in art and in everything that was going on that day in the Bargello, at least when it came to our random meeting. Still, the incredible thing was how much he physically excited me. I knew for sure that nothing but studying art would set my world on fire that day. He was a work of art himself, a walking, talking modern masterpiece. But my worst fear was looking like a quivering pile of clothing shrinking into nothing, so I kept talking to him, hoping he'd respond. "Do you study art here?"

"Me? No! I'm a day early for my new job and decided to take in some of Florence."

"What job would that be? Lawyer, accountant?"

"I'm a hydraulics engineer for Water-Vision. We're developing flood control measures to keep Florence's art and architecture safe . . ."

He went on, but I wasn't listening. Safe, huh? I wasn't but I didn't want the game to end. It dawned on me that I didn't even know the name of the man I was leading into infidelity, at least in my own mind. I extended my hand. "I'm Candy Buchanan." His hand felt sensually warm.

"And I . . . am late for an engagement." Quickly looking up at the clock and not giving me his name. I was flabbergasted! I wanted him, was willing to go out on a limb for him, sleep around behind Orlando's back, and he couldn't even give me a name? Maybe there was still one man on the face of the earth who saw a wedding ring as something still sacred and let it stand at that. That's why it was a ring in the first place, indicative of a circle of love. I should have respected that.

Apparently, he was the kind who went home to whomever had that matching ring.

But he was the one man I wanted. He was the most beautiful man I had ever seen.

I was not to be denied. He said his good-byes, and I watched him leave through the heavy iron doors, maybe never to be seen again. No way! I kicked into seduction mode again and casually walked out of the room.

I saw another museum door closing down the hall. My stranger was in there; I saw his sleeve just as the door closed. I picked up my pace, grabbed the door handle, and pulled it open. There my stranger was waiting inside for me. There were all kinds of beautiful masterpieces in there, but his gaze was on me. He smiled, his voice echoing throughout the room. "I knew you'd follow me."

He was damn right about that, but I wasn't crazy about his cockiness. I moved toward him, hands on my hips, staring that pretty dream-come-true in the face. I stopped directly before him, trying my best to ignore his sexual fragrance. "Say what?"

"I'm right, aren't I?" His tone was edgy, like he wanted to get to me. How the fuck could an insult be so sultry? His was, and it softened the blow of him being right. Still, I had to add my own edge. "Yeah, so? Okay, you're right. Now what?"

"You tell me, darling."

"Take it out," I said boldly.

"Why do you think I lured you in here? No one comes to this gallery."

"How do you know?"

"An affiliated company of ours is prepping it for renovation. And I have the key."

"Good for you. Lock us in, take it out, show me what I want."

He obeyed, then moved to face me. He had to be the prettiest man in captivity. Sorry, Orlando, but before reality truly struck me, I felt this stranger's hands on my dress, palming my already hardened buds, making me scorching hot. He bent and flicked his tongue across my clothed nipples, wetting the material in exquisite fashion. My body arched to the attention, getting what I was asking for but needing more, so I said again. "Show me what you have."

He pulled away from me. "You won't enjoy it until I get what I want."

My mouth went dry, my voice shook. "What . . . what is it that you want?"

"To taste you—my way. The minute I saw you, I knew I had to drag you back here, Mrs. Candy Buchanan. The sight of those barely-there panties under this incredibly luscious dress makes me crazy. And you know it, too."

"Sure as hell do."

"Then do I get what I want?"

"Don't ask; take it."

His lips met mine, sucking me, nibbling me into fits. His tongue snaked out, dancing with mine as his hands slid to my butt. Mercy, he squeezed it the same way Orlando did, hard, rugged, making me wet from the idea of him touching me. This stranger was making me feel like his lover by the mere touch of his large, warm hands.

The more he kissed me, the more my mind disolved. The way his mustache tickled my lips made me crazy, insane, free to be the wanton woman I wanted to be. So what? I was getting mine from the juiciest man alive, and my body was happy. My sex ached for him, practically begged for him through those tiny lacy panties. He heard it, heard me. My own voice murmured after a particularly succulent kiss. "Go deep on me, whoever you are."

"I'm the man who's going to burn those panties right off of you."

One more long draw on my mouth, then he licked up and down my cleavage, squeezing my breasts up and into plump orbs, leaving streaks between them. Just as I was beginning to entertain the idea of sliding my dress straps down for better access, he kissed down the front of my dress, resting one hand on my hips as his other lifted the hem. Exposed to him were panties easily peeled away from my wet skin, but instead, he kept kissing. His tiny nibbles started at the band of my panties, kissing just below my navel and working his way around the front of them. He soon moved to the leg area, kissing in detail as his other fingers massaged the wet seat, stroking it, rubbing hard. The other side got the same erotic attention as he kissed and rubbed his hard fingers into the wetness. The harder he stroked me, the more lavish his kisses became.

By that time, my hands were full of his curly dark hair, massaging his scalp, feeling his soft cheeks, feeling them move with each kiss he nailed me with. I was so ready to come that I was fuming. He knew it and tickled my seat with feathery strokes a little more. I called out to a stranger, not knowing what name to actually call him; "God" had to suffice.

He looked up at me. "At the boiling point, aren't you?"

"Pull them down, pretty boy, and taste me; lick your way into my body and taste heaven firsthand."

"Is that what you want?"

"It's what I need."

"I know what you need."

His hands grabbed my behind again, but with force, squeezing my cheeks together in vigorous motions. He enjoyed what he was doing to me, rocking my behind forward and backward, gaining momentum with his hand movements. His lips were now flush against the front of my panties, and he nibbled the center, yet didn't remove a single stitch. He just kept kissing, squeezing my behind to the tempo his lips were making with his hands. I could feel the sexual tension tighter and tighter within my core, wanting and needing release to this wonderful new lover. I knew he was going for that, but how, what way was his pleasure to heighten?

I called out again. "Take it! Eat me, baby. Eat me well." His tongue snaked out, licking my wet crotch through the thin material. He wanted the friction; it made his tongue hungry. The more he licked my soaking wet labia, the harder he thrust my buttocks against him. I could feel his tongue swirling around, wanting entrance, yet refraining himself from the ultimate temptation. The wet material, along with his tongue, moved into me, tickling my clit and lips, making me weak, making me so ready to deliver what I knew he wanted to take.

I couldn't hold out any longer, but he continued to eat, and ate well. The more my nectar spilled, the more vigorous his tongue action became, stroking me from front to back as he moaned, making hungry sounds and talking as he devoured my cream. "Baby, this is so fucking good. Keep rocking against me, girl. Rock harder, let me lick more . . . that's right, like that! Give it to me."

His tongue darted across the cotton seat so fast that I screamed out, grabbed my breasts in my hands, reared back, and released more to him. My body pounded more for this stranger than for my own husband, but I was beyond caring about that. What would he be like inside of me—tongue, penis, everything? What could he make my body do that no other man had ever managed? He'd already done it, taking me to the limits without the benefit of showing me one single inch of his body.

He delivered his last lick, catching every drop, then slowly stood and faced me. We kissed once again, then he pulled away. No words, no anything. My hands hung on to his damp, sweat-stained shirt, feeling his heat but wanting to see it.

After his kiss, however, he backed away from me and walked to the entrance. Before I could speak, he disappeared behind the door.

Damn! I was hoping for more afternoon delight before having lunch and going home to cook for Orlando, but I decided to screw all of that. When a man gets into your blood, you've gotta get 'em.

I had to follow him. I caught his scent like a tracking dog would, and nothing would do until I got the rest of what I needed to have. Whoever he was, he wasn't finished; he knew it and so did I.

The sun baked my wet skin the minute I hit the street, but I couldn't think about anything other than that pretty man now walking down the street and out of my life. My clit was still vibrating because of him, and I could barely walk. Adding insult to injury, the stilettos were beginning to pinch like crazy. I hadn't planned on being in them long, only to go to the market, take in an exhibit, and lunch. I found myself doing way more, like trotting down the damn marbled streets, almost twisting my ankles just to get to a man I had no business with, but he treated me so well that I had to have more. Whoever he was, he was worth the torture. By the end of the day, I expected to be tortured in more exotic ways. He liked me, and I knew it, liked how I tasted. The smile on his face after he licked me to death told me that!

The more he walked, strutting that tight butt of his, the hotter I got. The midday sun was so steamy that I could see the print of his back against his now-wet silk shirt. Hints of tight muscles rippled everywhere; the deep curve of his back tapering down to slender hips and tight behind was hazardous to my senses.

He kept walking, and I kept pace despite shoes I was all but ready to fling into the gutter. You know how it is, the shoes can be killers, but if they look good and are eye-catching to men, the things stay on. I endured it, solely for the hunt, and what a grand one it was. The prey was absolutely mouth-watering.

On occasions, his head turned just to see if his personal sex slave was still there. I was. Where the hell else would I be, home rattling pots and pans? True enough that that was where I should have been, but I wasn't. I had accepted my fate.

He kept walking. I kept following, and we walked right past the other place I was supposed to got to that day, another museum. I looked down at my watch, a half hour before my lunch date. I seriously didn't think I'd be able to attend since I was following my lunch down the street. Denise would have to go it alone. If she laid one eye on the entrée I was following, she'd surely understand why I was standing her ass up.

My throat was so dry and my nerves completely shot from not getting the rest of what I needed, yet there was no fucking way I was going to stop. I was on a mission.

Finally, my stranger had mercy on me and ducked into a quaint little side bar. And wasn't it just perfect, something you'd see in one of those artsy movies that your mother told you never to watch—especially in the company of a man. The hell with that. I wanted to star in one of those forbidden flicks with him.

La Lourage was noted for its fine Italian wines and a was personal favorite of Denise's. She told me to check out everything, especially the cafés and sidewalk liquor houses. I'd never seen anything like them.

What I wanted was to be at the outdoor café, pretend I was an authentic Italian, sipping wine, looking fly with a carafe of wine, eyeing my stranger's cock on the sly. Don't all true Italians in lovely Florence get their share of wine and sex at the same time? Why not me?

My stranger went inside, as did I, chucking the outdoor daydream in a freakin' heartbeat. The inside was just as appealing. Fine gondola paintings on the walls, chandeliers made of the prettiest cut glass, and a fat Italian man behind the bar, welcoming my stranger with a firm, friendly hand-shake. They knew each other, were probably best buddies. Yes, my stranger was a man about town who went every-where, did everything—probably did every woman he could get his hands on. So what? I was glad to be a notch on his belt. I wasn't supposed to be anywhere else in the world but there.

I had no idea what the men were discussing, didn't actu-ally give a damn, so I waited at the entrance in anticipation of what erotic fantasy my stranger had in store for me. He turned around and pointed to me with a delicious smile on his face. The bartender smiled as well, big and wide. The two shook hands again, and my stranger waited for his friend to pour a carafe of what looked to be sangria and crushed ice. But where were the glasses? Mr. Gorgeous walked into the back room, assuming I would soon join him.

My staying power was diminishing, though his certainly wasn't. I wanted him to nail me and get it over with before I had to go home to a lonely apartment. I slowly pushed the swinging door open and saw him standing near in front of a table, holding the carafe. A smile as enticing as the rest of his fine self lured me.

I was standing at the door, waiting for permission to ap-proach him when he called out to me. "What do you need, an invitation? Lock that door behind you. You know why you're here, so come and get it."

His words were blunt, but truthful. Yes, I was there to get fucked. No flowery words, just the nitty-gritty, getting fucked! I slowly approached him, stopping inches from him; he was still the most beautiful thing I'd ever laid eyes on. The sun was shining in from a stained-glass window, illuminating his already golden complexion, making him sexier than God had originally planned. I couldn't wait. I knew he was going to give all that golden deliciousness to me. He was ready.

So was I.

He took my face into the palms of his hands and kissed

me. His tongue entered me, wetting my dry lips with stroke after stroke, making my own tongue dance with his. It was raw, wicked and dirty, the way he danced around inside my mouth. His hands squeezed my butt again, forcing me into that fiery rocket between his thighs. He was killing me by making me wait for what I wanted, yet my arms encircled his neck and shoulders, pressing farther into him for anything I could possibly get. I rubbed against him, sliding my hand down his rippled chest and onto that giant cock. It felt good in my hands, natural, as if he was supposed to be fondled by me. Almost insane from want, I broke away from him. "What are you going to do to me?"

"Everything."

He lay me down on the sturdy table and looked at me. "You must want a lot to follow a stranger around Florence."

"I only want what I have coming to me."

"And what would that be?"

"A good, stiff fuck. You started this, and now you have to finish it."

"I didn't start this, Candy. You started it by wearing that damn sexy-ass dress."

"What would you prefer me wear, nothing?"

"Yes."

"Then take care of it."

He leaned over me with the carafe in his hands, stuck one finger into the sangria, and traced my lips with it. He kissed it off, then fingered the buttons on the front of my dress. The minute he got to the second button, my hands stopped his. "Why haven't you told me your name?"

"Because I don't need to. When you want raw, turbo-charged sex, names matter very little, right?"

"I guess."

"Besides, you may know my wife. She's a pretty hot item around Italy. What I do, I do in secrecy. I do that because I'm a man of means, by no means. But I am rated M."

"For what?"

"Massive."

I reached down and cupped his scrotum, bounced it in my hand, feeling the weight and intensity of it. That same hand worked north, spanning the length of his shaft. A good ten-incher if I'd ever felt one. "Massive, huh?"

"Damn straight!"

"Let me see it."

"In due time. I get mine first."

"You got yours already."

"I want more." He set the carafe down and quickly unfastened the rest of the buttons on my dress, reached behind me, and unhooked my bra. He lifted the bra over my breasts and looked down. Desire filled those deep, dark eyes, his tongue gracefully moistened his full lips, and his hands automatically started massaging my breasts. He squeezed the tight, pointed buds between his thumbs and forefingers, rubbing them in circles until they stood up for him.

I continued to watch him as he manipulated my nipples. He was like a child on his birthday, smiling glassy-eyed at the biggest package. My hands covered his as he moved them across my soft flesh. "You like them, don't you."

"Can't you tell by this stiff rod?"

"Then taste them. They're reaching out to you, Mr. Stranger. That's your new name since you won't tell me who you really are."

"I'm a stranger to any woman I take in broad daylight."

"Then this is a habit with you?"

"It is, but you're the only one I'm addicted to."

"Why me?"

"Because you radiate sex, strong, earthy, delicious sex; the only kind of sex that sets me off." He took the carafe and slowly dripped the sangria across my nipples, dowsing them, cooling my hot skin. The cool liquid streaked my sides as it rolled from my taut breasts. He poured more, massaging it in, watching as it trickled down my chest and stomach, dipping into my navel, wetting the band of my panties.

The feel of it on my body was delicious. I never knew wine tasted better wearing it. It got better! My stranger's hands were full of wine and breasts, moving them up and down, toying with me as his rod got stiffer and stiffer. He leaned against me, kissed my neck and collarbone, then worked his way down. He was like an animal suddenly, licking and lapping me. His tongue and lips circled my breasts, mellowing in the flavor of sangria-painted flesh. His lips pulled and tugged at my nipples, and he raked his teeth across them, rolling them between his fingers and tongue, doing double duty on me.

My back arched to the sensations. My legs wrapped around his hips, feeling that M-for-massive hard-on as it pushed against me. I called to him, screamed for him to release it and let it play at my opening. He ignored my words and continued to work his magic on my breasts. His licks were slow and methodical. Long strokes dampened my chest and stomach, getting every molecule of sangria left on me. His tongue swirled into my navel, drinking the drops inside it.

He raised briefly to pour more wine on to his fingers, letting the liquid drip from them, long enough to engulf a hot, squirming punanny into a sensual explosion. I stared into his super sexy face. "What are you gonna do with the rest of that wine?"

"You'll find out."

Long fingers moved to the leg of my panties and pulled them aside. What awaited him was a quivering, feverish, throbbing sex just waiting for riotous action. I wanted that beautiful stranger to slide those fingers so deeply into me that I'd feel him invading me forever. I wanted his lips, tongue, everything pulling at me, spreading my core open and eating it tenderly, passionately.

He knew what I wanted, what I needed, and he did just that. He played my labia until it hummed. I clawed at his soft hands. "Do it! Spread me; fuck me."

He smiled at me. "Isn't that what you'd love? To have a big, fat, juicy rod taking you to another time zone?"

"That's what I want."

"It's all about what I want. Remember that." He dampened his fingers again, then slowly dipped two into my sex. There was a bit of a tingle but he soothed it by rocking slowly in and out. A third finger slid in, taking up the same rhythm as the other two. My clit throbbed mercilessly as his fingers slid around it. My back arched as I screamed out to a man who had no name. It was so good to me. No man had ever rocked my body the way this lover did.

I could not resist. All I could do I was go with the flow and enjoy everything I could possibly get away with. And if it was in the cards to follow this man into the wilderness of unbridled lust and downright dirty sex—so be it. The day was mine, maybe the night as well if my plan was indeed a workable plan.

My secret stud worked me hard, sliding his fingers deeply into me as I watched his face, a wildly sexy face, so beautiful as he nailed me. Sweat dripped from his smooth brown forehead and mixed with the sangria on my chest. He parted my legs farther, slamming more and more of his fingers into my sopping core.

He leaned over me again, licking and tasting my almost dewy breasts and nipples, making them wet again. My cries made him wilder, and he stroked me harder until my muscles clenched around his fingers. He felt my orgasm, tugged at me more to intensify it. His fingers squeezed my clit, feeling it tremble, and he smiled a smile of satisfaction. His voice tickled my still-perky nipples. "Girl, you come so damn good, like no other woman."

I had to. He hadn't even penetrated me with his shaft, yet. I was ready, willing, and able to do anything he wanted me to. "How many times would I be able to have you? Every day, every hour, or maybe once a month?"

"Every day. My wife wouldn't care."

"Why would she not care when she has someone as good as you are?"

"How good is Orlando? Aren't you doing the same to him?"

I rose up and stiffened at the accusation. "What do you know about Orlando?"

He pushed me back down. "My point, Candy, do you want me enough to keep doing what we're doing? I don't care about Orlando. I don't even know who he is, other than a coworker I haven't met yet."

"Haven't met yet? You wouldn't tell him if you ever met him, would you?"

"I just said I don't care about him."

"Well I do, but I care more about getting mine."

"Doesn't he give you yours?"

"Yes, but I want more, plain and simple! Give me what I want, and I'll hang around."

He patted his still stiff phallus. "You mean this?"

"You got it!"

"No, you got it, and if you want it, you'll do what I ask."

"What are you asking?"

"For the thrill of a longer chase."

"How can I give you a longer chase, which could last months if I don't know your name?"

"Create one for me."

"I have—the perfect stranger."

"Good enough, because that's exactly what I am to you and to other women."

"After this day, will I be your only conquest?"

He winked at me. "You are the best I've had. I couldn't handle you along with anyone else. Alone you'll probably kill me."

I stroked his sweaty pecs. "Sexual death is a blast. You'll eventually thank me for killing you."

He pulled my dress apart again, exposing my sticky breasts.

He moistened the cloth laying on he table next to the carafe and smoothed it against my warm skin, diluting the sangria and sweat that blanketed my body.

His soothing cloth circled my nipples, which still burned for his lips. He wiped in circular motions down my chest and stomach before wrapping the cloth around his finger. My head raised. "What are you going to do with that?"

"Something good."

I didn't know what to expect but, whatever it was, I was up for it. I watched as he dipped the cloth-covered finger into the water, letting it drip across my panties, sliding the leg band away. He dipped the cloth into my sex, massaged my folds and clit with it, soothing, soothing me. What was it about this man? Who was he really? Again, my head lifted. "Who are you? Tell me the truth."

"I'm your perfect stranger, remember?"

"Don't make me ask you again?"

"Then stop asking." He saw my bewildered expression. "The truth? Okay. I'm someone you'll love."

"I already love you."

He took my hand and sat me up on the table. "You don't love me yet." He placed my hand around his bulging zipper. "When you've had this, then you'll be in love. Take my word for it." He backed away from me. "Do you want to be in love?"

"Yes."

"Then button your dress and follow me."

"Another disappearing act?"

He didn't answer, just left me to pull myself together.

Once outside, the heat baked me again. I looked at my watch again; it was almost one in the afternoon and I had done nothing but get halfway screwed by a stranger. Orlando's dinner should have been on the stove, his wine chilling instead of his *wife* wearing it. Where were his flowers that the famous Carlo Vinucci had handpicked? Waiting for some lucky woman to pick them up because I wouldn't be back for them, not that day. Someone else would be the thankful recipient.

I followed behind my lover. But where was he taking me? Wherever it was, he knew I'd follow, because I was weak for him. He had girth to kill for, divorce for. Damn, what had I become, a human sex toy? Yes! His!

The streets were now populated with working men and women out for lunch. Children were running and playing; others were going to the midtown festival to gather their flowers and wine for a romantic evening. What would I have for Orlando? Burned veal because it would have to be cooked in a hurry, if it was made at all. Would I even be home for him? I was on a journey to sex heaven, and the pilot was right before me, leading me to a big billowy cloud to await a big, thick cock!

He led me to the river, flagged down a gondola and stepped aboard. He told the navigator to wait, knowing I'd be stepping inside almost immediately.

I approached the boat, and he held out his hand and brought me over the waters of the Arno. I sat across from him, staring into his big eyes. My body was still tingling from him, aching for him, ready for whatever. "What now?"

He slid over to me and opened the door to the small cabin just right for lovers. "Arch your back and lean against the seat."

I did it. My legs were wide open, facing him. He moved to his knees and placed my legs over his shoulders. "You ready?"

"For what?"

"More tongue, more fingers, more licking."

"What I want is your length inside me."

"In due time."

"Stop saying that."

"Don't ask again. I told you this is my show. I'm in control here, and I call the shots. It has to be that way, Candy."

"I suppose you are right, since beggars can't be choosers."

"Are you begging for it?"

"Do you want me to?"

He shrugged his shoulders nonchalantly. "Sure, why not? I love it when women scream and ask for it. The gondolier won't hear or understand—this is our secret."

"Is that what it would take to feel that hot, hard member of yours?"

"Time can only tell; now relax and enjoy the waves—both kinds." He pulled at my panties until they slid past my stilettos. I watched as he licked the crotch over and over before sliding them into his pocket.

"A souvenir?" I inquired.

"No, darling. My souvenir is right here." He toyed and pulled at my almost hairless crotch and rubbed his finger up and down on it. He wrapped his hands around my thigh and scooted me deeper into him, arched my back a bit more, then licked me. I knew it was going to be good. The way his tongue danced in my mouth was the same way he was dancing within my sex. He swirled, tugged, nipped, and gently bit all around my clit. I was crazy from pleasure. The man poling the gondola could have heard all kinds of sounds, shrieks, and cries, because my stranger was eating me the way he did at the café.

I was getting a French kiss from my anus to my stomach, covering every spot. I could feel his skillful mouth moving up and down on me. He was taming a wicked-wild punanny, getting me to the point where I would only do and say what he wanted. He was controlling me, turning me into someone I didn't know, didn't want to know. Who was I? A lover like no other.

For the fifth time since that morning, I came. I spilled nectar all over him, drenching his mouth, his delicious mustache, but he just kept eating, gripping my thigh tighter with one hand as he reached between his legs for something. He never stopped with the pleasure. The more I came, the harder he forced his lips into my labia. His fingers matched what his lips were doing, winding me, plucking me until I heard his own cries. He bucked against me, gripped me tighter, spread my thighs to either side of the boat, braced himself, then came into his hand.

I could see nothing until he rested against his seat, worn out and out of breath, his chest heaving up and down frantically. His sexy face was flushed, and smiling. I stroked his cheeks. "Was it good, baby?"

"Not as good as it will get."

I looked between his parted thighs and saw his pants gaping open with the thickest, strongest erection standing to my attention. It was everything I dreamed it would be, and the only thing that occupied my mind from that point on was stroking it, making it bigger, stiffer, rocking my hand up and down on it. He grabbed his exposed phallus and jerked it slowly. His eyes returned to me. "Help me with this."

"You mean you'll let me touch it?"

"But only a certain way. Like this. Watch and take notes on how to completely please me, because you'll be doing a lot of this."

The faster his hand moved on it, the weaker I became. I'd never felt like that before over the mere sight of a man, but he wasn't your average man; he was beautiful everywhere, from his eyes and dark curly hair to his fine Italian croc shoes.

I needed something to cool my senses because he sure wasn't doing it. I reached for the water bottle in my bag, dribbled some into my hand and patted my face, letting the water refresh me before gripping his tool; a tool I knew would take both of my hands to master.

I brought him to another climax, watching thick, creamy come spurt from his hulking cock. What dazzled me was watching it run down the sides of his shaft, like erupting lava from a volcano. I wanted to taste him, lick him, but he refused me, using his same line: "Not yet. There's more to come."

We reached the docks, and he returned my panties and helped me to land, making sure the wind didn't lift my dress and expose me to the world. Thus our chase continued down the streets of Florence. I was hungry for both him and food, and so was he. We stopped at a street vendor where he purchased a cream-filled pastry for himself and an Italian sausage for me. I made him watch me slowly devour the length of the hot meat. He watched with enthusiasm, licking the velvety cream from his lips while continuing to watch me. When my last inch of meat was gone, he dabbed at my mouth with a hanky, saying, "When it's my turn, I expect the same thing or back to Orlando you will go."

Whoever this man was, he was sure to get pleased by me and in secrecy. I was up for all the secrecy possible. It only made the game hotter and wilder. I wanted my stranger too much not to do it.

This man walked me more blocks, to where I had no idea. We passed the restaurant where I was to have met Denise almost a half hour ago. I walked past the entrance a little faster in case she was still there waiting but was not fast enough. Denise saw me as she walked out. My stranger looked back to me as if to dare me to stop and explain. He wanted no one seeing the two of us together. Neither did I. As I passed Denise, I put my fingers to my lips to hush her, praying she'd keep a secret and not let on to anyone that she'd seen me. Denise watched me traipse behind this beautiful stranger, and simply shrugged her shoulders, gripped her bottle of port a little tighter, then walked in the opposite direction. I was thankful. Denise was cool enough to keep her mouth shut.

I kept my pace with the beautiful one but was becoming weary. The coochie was still in need of deep satisfaction, but the high heels were killing me, yet I walked. *Where the fuck is he taking me? To hell and back?* Indeed he was. There was a smoking pit somewhere with my name on it, but I was glad to jump in the fire, so long as it was his. That's how much release I needed and was crazy enough to attain it any way I could.

After seven long blocks of cobblestone streets, he had mercy on me and ducked into a five-story building. I lost him. Still determined, I went in and tried to find him, searching corners, stairwells, then, finally, I could hear him climbing the steps. I couldn't reach him because he was too high up. He kept climbing, and I kept trying to keep pace while those red stilettos pinched me. I reached the top and saw a single door standing ajar. I just knew he was now in his wife's apartment, and he had the nerve to take another woman in there. Sure, he had the guts—after all, this was a man sneaking around on his wife and in broad daylight. What made him even bolder was that he was Orlando's coworker. One wrong move on my part and I was history.

I pushed the door open and saw him standing across the room with a smug look on his face. Man, he was godly. Had the Lord made anything prettier, he'd surely have kept it up there with him. When I stepped through the door, he was leaning on a railing with his shirt unbuttoned. Caramel-brown skin glistened against his pale yellow shirt. He was a high degree of perfection; rippled pecs with hard, dark brown nipples dotting his chest. I prayed to see more of him, wanting to stroke that gorgeous chest, but I wasn't allowed to.

My eyes lowered to the taut muscles dimpling his abdomen, then down to the dent in his stomach that housed a navel just ready for my tongue to slide across. All I could do was stare and smile—a wicked smile that practically begged to eat him.

His voice caught me off guard, that sexy voice again; a voice a woman could fuck to every minute of the day, every day of the week. Though he had spoken to me many times before, it was something about being secluded with him, in a forbidden zone, a dangerous zone that could very possibly house a wife hidden behind any corner. Did I care? You know I probably didn't.

He held out his hand, saying, "Are you going to just stand there, or are you going to get over here and let me slide something thick and hot into you?"

"Finally."

"You knew the rules and agreed to them willingly. Am I correct?"

"You are."

"Then get over here and get what you've been imagining."

"Where's your wife?"

"Why do you care?"

"I care because she could still be here. I'll admit to being your slut, but I'd like to remain a living one. Knives in my back aren't exactly a thrill."

"She's in Rome for the day, checking out a new museum."

"What does she do?"

"She gets the hell out of my face so I can have my privacy; though she actually has no idea what I do with that privacy. Does that answer your question?"

"It'll suffice."

"Then *suffice* me. I'm ready to spill the goods."

"More than what you did on the boat? You spilled a lot."

"That depends on you and what you do to work me."

As I approached him, I looked around at a room that opened into a penthouse patio. The sun drenched walls were adorned with valuable, richly colored painting, all of female nudes, something I desperately needed to be, but for him only.

He took my hands and pulled me into him. I swear the closer he moved into me, the larger his shaft looked poking through already unzipped pants. The very sight of that hulking erection made me slide my panties to my ankles. He watched with wildness in his eyes, then reached down for the skimpy panties, brought them to his lips and licked the crotch again. His only words were, "Umm! You taste like vanilla pudding—rich, creamy, and lickable. Just thought I'd mention that if I hadn't already."

"You hadn't."

"You know you followed me seven blocks just to have your panties licked—again."

"We did that, and I definitely plan to have you do more

than taste panties. I plan to have you taste me again, but with that pipe in your pants. Now that I've seen it, you can't take it from me. I'd have you killed."

"I plan to do the killing. Ready to die?"

"I've been ready."

He moved into the crook of my neck, tickling me with his tongue. "Damn! You're too boss, girl. And I know for sure exactly how boss you are, especially in a certain place."

I tipped his chin back down to meet me. "Consider me your personal Candy store."

"And you're open for business."

"It's my grand opening, and every inch of that wonderful rod you finally showed me is surely invited."

He led me to a chaise lounge in the corner of the patio, where I proceeded to remove my dress. After it fell in a crumpled heap at my feet, I laid back on the lounge looking up at him. My hand reached out for him. "Let me do you, mystery man."

"Sure you can handle it? It's what you'll be screaming for the entire night, lovely one, so get prepared."

I wrapped my hand around the prettiest mass I'd ever seen—beautiful, thick, and ready to screw the heck out of me. I couldn't believe I had him in my hands again, and not for just brief moments. I could take him all afternoon and night. His wife was in Rome, and my Orlando was wherever. I could play on my new playground and let him dip his shovel into my sand all night long. I was aching from the idea of it. I was finally going to get it, have him nail me in ways I've only imagined thus far.

My hand slowly stroked his tip, squeezing its moisture, then down to the wonderful veins rippling from it. I could come just over how it felt in my hand. The moment I looked at him, I knew he'd feel smooth and sexy like that. Someone as fine as he was couldn't have been any other way.

When he took his shirt completely off and exposed those rippling shoulder muscles, I could feel myself slowly losing it again. I placed his hand back on my breast and uttered in a quivering voice, "Do me now. Let me slide your pants down and go for it."

He feathered his fingers around my hardened nipples, then down my stomach, and said in a dry, seductive voice, "No. A chick like you needs to be done slowly."

I knew I was in for it then because he got harder by hearing his own words. Still, he didn't remove his pants. He wanted me to desire him even more, to get me to the breaking point, but the self-restraint wasn't easy.

He retrieved his tie from the floor and wrapped it around my wrists, knotting it on the back of the lounge. I was now powerless for him to do any wicked thing he chose. I couldn't wait to see what he had in store for the punanny.

He started at my forehead and kissed his way down to my lips. He straddled me, hovering above me, yet every delicious thing on him was still out of my reach. It was frustrating, yet so provocative. He dipped into me, slowly moving his tongue across my lower lip, then my top, teasing me mercilessly.

From there his tongue made love to mine, building my intensity, making my core crave his cock, filling me completely. He licked down to my neck and breasts, sucking hard on each one, filling his mouth with my plump mounds. How I wanted him to release my hands, as well as that erotic swelling between my thighs. He kept the torture going until I was about ready to faint. His massive, hard member was pressing against my stomach as he worked his way down my body. I screamed out, "Pleeasse!" He didn't stop until his cheek was pressed against the inside of my left thigh, getting more of what he'd had all day long.

His arms wrapped around my thighs, slightly lifting my buttocks for better leverage. I've never been hoisted that high before, not even on the boat. Lifting me that high was marvelous beyond human thought. He licked the sweetness away while teasing the perimeter of my labia.

My back arched from the pleasure as his tongue danced

around my mound. Then he dipped inside, over and over again, licking, nibbling, tugging. He did it so perfectly, making me squirm from sheer desire. I started screaming like he said I would. And just when he thought I was wasted, he withdrew the tongue, leaving me breathless and gasping for air while talking. "What the heck are you doing?"

"Something you didn't expect; now stay quiet."

I watched as he left the room. Maybe he was leaving me alone to fantasize. But I started thinking instead. *Suppose his wife walks in and catches me like this. Damn! She could easily return from Rome and surprise him. A man like this is worth cutting a trip short just to get back to his cock.* I almost panicked at the idea of it. "Get the heck back in here. Don't leave me alone!"

There was nothing. The place was still, and I was in there in the middle of the room, tied up and naked. I called to him again. "Where are you? This is so not fair."

I saw a doorknob turn on the other door, and it scared me. But what the hell, life was life and thus far, I'd lived mine on the edge.

He peeked through the door. "Good, you're nice and scared, aren't you?"

"Why would you do that to me? Are you getting me back for following a strange man home?"

"Not exactly. I like sex that's tight and trembling; makes for the best friction."

"You ass! Get over here and finish me."

He stepped through the door with something behind his back. There was a devilish grin on his face. "You ready for something cool?"

I twisted and tried jerking out of my bondage. "I hope what you're talking about is putting on the air-conditioning."

"Think again. I know it's hot, baby, but I've got something way better than air-conditioning."

"Like what?"

"Close your eyes."

"No!" He was *really* beginning to scare me.

"Close your eyes. I won't hurt you. I promise. I haven't brought you this far to hurt you."

I was reluctant but did what he said.

"Spread your legs farther apart."

Though I was scared, that sounded way too tempting to me. I just knew the banana from his fruit bowl now had a better job than to look appetizing on a table. I relaxed my thighs and calmed down after realizing that this was fantasy, pure, hot and real enough to make me lose my mind. I felt his fingers between my legs again, separating my folds, rubbing his fingers up and down on my clit. My stomach heaved up and down; my lips got dry. "Please."

"It's coming, Candy."

His juicy lips licked my punanny, sucking it like crazy. He hummed, "Ready for the ultimate?"

"From the minute I laid my eyes on you."

He reached within his napkin and pulled out something.

"What do you have?"

"Something incredible. You'll love it."

I felt something cool and wet against my core—ice. My back arched to the cool, hot pleasure he fed into me. "What the hell is that?"

"An ice shaft."

"Let me see it."

There it was, seven inches of iced cock, carved almost exactly the way my stranger looked to me. "Like it, honey?"

"That's incredible. Slide it in."

He kissed my lips once more before I felt that long, cool member pulsate through my opening. The pleasure of it was so intoxicating that my back arched higher. He gently moved it in and out, then picked up pace as our excitement grew. The more he rocked it, the more it dripped into me, melting me and it at the same time.

Watching that iced shaft nail me made him so hot and hard that he pulled his own out and matched the ice stroke per stroke. I asked him not to explode unless he was inside of me, but I didn't know if he could hold off any longer.

He grabbed the ice, brought it to my lips, and watched me suck it. That almost brought his house down, but I dared him not to release. He was a good listener.

His eyes narrowed as he watched me swallowing the melting liquid. "You really want it, don't you?"

I couldn't speak, couldn't think; all I could do was watch him as he stepped out of those beige pants. He was so buff, even his muscled thighs were pretty; but his length was prettier and, yes, a ten-incher. He straddled the chair so that each of his thighs was on either side of me. He slowly fed that delicious erection to my waiting mouth inch by inch. I was so full of him that I thought I'd died and gone to hard-on Heaven. His scrotum tightened, and I so wanted to feel his balls in my hands, but he did me one better. He pulled out and let my tongue have at them. I teased them, nibbled them until he was just about ready.

His body lowered to mine, placing his shaft at my very opening as he teased again, "Maybe we should just stop and let you beg more for it."

That was when I screamed at the top of my lungs, "No! Give it to me—now."

He winked. "Guess you have suffered enough."

"Damn straight I have. I've followed your tight ass all over the place, let you drink from my body, tease me, make me crazy with sex. Now you want to tell me I haven't suffered enough? What do you have waiting for me, your wife? Would she like to join us and get her fucking kicks also?"

"Shut up! Don't talk about her like that."

"I'm not the one cheating on her!"

"No, the only thing you get to do right now is take all of me."

I could feel him poking at my wet folds and I screamed again, "Untie me and let me touch you."

He got into his rhythm and screwed me for a good five

minutes. It was marvelous, everything I imagined it would be. His wet, thick joint plundered through me, stimulating my juiced folds. I was begging for him to go deeper instead of simply teasing my opening. "Please, release me. I just want to touch you. I've barely gotten that chance today, touching you only when *you* wanted me to."

"Why should I let you be free? You're out of control"

"Because if you let me touch you the way I want to, you'll never want another woman."

"I knew that the minute I saw you in the museum."

"Then satisfy me."

"Fine, you want release, you'll get it."

Once my hands were free, they ravaged every part of him, playing in his thick dark curls, moving down his back, rippled sides, muscles in his upper arms. The only thought I had was how strong those arms were, how they could embrace me. We tumbled to the carpeting, but he stayed inside of me. I whispered to him in a quivering voice, "I want all of you inside of me." He did, and slid that cock into almost every crevice I owned. I'd never tried anal sex before. Orlando always said it was unnatural. But me, I was the daring one, always had been and was ready to try anything.

My rowdy, rough stranger flipped me onto my stomach, forcing my knees under my chin as he spread my butt apart. He slid in so slowly and expertly, making my muscles wrap around his shaft and pull, stretch, making it harder and stiffer. He just kept pushing it in and out, nailing me like it was the end of days. But it never hurt. He was all about pleasure—intense pleasure.

After squeezing the tip of that delicious cock with everything inside me, his white cream spilled and saturated me. It was so warm and oozing between my fingers and behind, and I was happy to massage it in completely.

He collapsed onto my back while his still-erect member hid safely inside my body. I wanted more of him because I still wasn't completely satisfied. He'd started this mess by seducing me in the first damn place, so there was no way he was going to tire out.

I took his hand into mine and slid it across my dripping sex. "Feel how hot it is for you? It's even hotter inside, but if you're tired—"

"Who the hell said I was tired?" He kissed my lips once again, letting his tongue coil around my thirsty mouth, matching my rhythms like the expert he was, anticipating my every move.

As his tongue sexed out my mouth, his body moved between my legs. His arms wrapped around my thighs, hoisting them higher, making our parts fit together at just the right axis for deep penetration. I'd been waiting for that all afternoon.

When his tip met with my opening again, I looked at him. "Don't you dare tease me. I want it all, shoved into me, pounding away at me, quaking my body like Mt. St. Helens. "Boy, I want molten rock spewing from you and covering me. You understand me, Mr. Stranger of my wildest fucking dreams?"

Not a word. He gripped me tighter, standing practically on his knees as he guided that monstrously strong, deep hose into me, rocking his hips with every inch he fed me. As he guided himself inside, I watched his face tense, enjoying the sensations my swollen walls was supplying him. He looked like he could feel everything as he pumped heavily into me.

His strokes got so good to me that I could feel the tension churning in my body, revving me up for an orgasm that would surely drive me crazy. Fine. I knew I was crazy in the first damn place. Why not go out with a bang, right? That's what I got, a bang. He banged so stiffly and precisely into my honey that my head was swimming. When I looked at him, I saw the most miraculous thing to hit my imagination since sex toys. Hell, he was better than any sex gadget invented. My stranger was the ultimate sex toy of the frickin' universe. Way to go, man without a name.

He rocked me a good fifteen minutes straight, no interruptions, no stopping for commercial breaks, just straight, unadulterated, creamy, steamy cock feeding me to the hilt!

The more I screamed out to him, the harder he pumped into me. Again, my hands left red marks on his arms and wrists. I barely got out a few words. "Your wife—she won't even remember giving those to you."

"She'll have her memories, take my word for it. You see, I have to do this all over again tonight. Tonight is our anniversary." He pumped in harder and harder as he continued his wicked words. "For right now, this is my gift to myself, eating and slamming the most beautiful woman I've ever seen in my life."

The pressure in my body released and I screamed to the top of my lungs, yet he pumped more, more. Mercy!

My body, wiggling hurriedly and ecstatically under his, made him come. The fountain turned on, spewing, drenching my insides just the way I wanted him to. I got what I wanted finally, total saturation and from the sexiest man.

By the time he finished with me, three hours had passed. He rolled back on top of me, pinning my hands back down saying, "Did you like what you waited all day for?"

My eyes stared deeply into his. "Yes." I stared deeper. "One question. Who the hell are you, really?"

"A man who loves to please his woman.

"You didn't answer my question."

"Then tell me you enjoyed what I did to you, and I'll tell you who I am.

"Done deal. You know I loved every second of it. I told you it was fucking out of this world."

He kissed my cheek, then reared back and smiled. "Well then, happy anniversary girl. I wanted to give you something special, not just the usual box of candy and flowers. We should play games like this all the time."

I quickly kissed his smiling lips. "Orlando Buchanan, you have the imagination of a mad man. I wasn't sure about this game when you mentioned it last night, but after thinking about it, I figured it would be fun, different. You really had me going, boy, playing my body until it hummed for you— only you, Orlando."

"That was my idea, baby. The closer we got to our anniversary I noticed your demeanor though you tried hiding it. You wanted to run wild, and I wanted to make it happen the only way I could. I figured playing a game and letting you explore your fantasy would be fun. You wanted to be enticed by a stranger, and you played it perfectly."

"Acting like you didn't know was a little frightening, especially the way you talked to me at times, but it was well worth it. Damn, Orlando, I could never really cheat on you. You're my world.

"And, you're mine, all mine." He snapped his fingers. "And it's time."

"For what? Another iced cock?"

"Nope."

I watched my real *perfect stranger* run buck-naked from the room and duck into the kitchen. I heard the refrigerator door open and saw the light flash on, wondering what other sexy treat he had in store. Whatever it was, nothing compared to having Orlando's love. He was all I needed.

Orlando ran back in holding a bottle of prosecco with a big yellow ribbon on its neck. "I forgot one very special thing, baby—toasting to the best wife a man could have."

"You really mean that, don't you?"

"I mean every word when it comes to you."

"Well, like you said, it's our anniversary. You should have dipped the iced cock in sparkling wine and fed it to me. That cold item was oh-so-hot. Where'd it come from?"

"You can get anything online. I had about thirty of them delivered in dry ice, one for every day of the month. Don't you ever look in the freezer?"

"Apparently not today. I put the bottle in and left." My

fingers grazed his cheek. "Pour it on me anyway if you like. Make me wet. Orlando—everywhere. Make me your iced queen."

"You're already my queen"

"A queen who has a king who skips work to screw beautiful American women. Good thing there wasn't that other woman behind a wall waiting to kill me."

"Girl, you're the only queen in my palace and you were so worth me asking my new boss for one more day before starting work.

"So, when do you really start work?"

"Tomorrow, but tonight is still young. More prosecco, Candy-girl?"

"Yes and in all the right places."

He slowly drizzled the cool liquid on my breasts and worked his way down. . .

Six AM *the next morning.*

I awakened with a smile on my face and a sore body from being satisfied until two that morning. Five whole years of not ever wanting to look at another man other than my precious Orlando was a real accomplishment. There was one sad part to my fairytale story, however—no call from home to congratulate me. But the only thing that really truly mattered was what Orlando thought of me. To him, I was nothing but sweet perfection.

He's the same to me. I looked over at the slumbering sex machine I called a husband and nestled under his arm. He was wonderful, glorious, and every inch the wild man I'd always wanted. My eyes closed, taking advantage of the one hour I had left before having to get up.

I rested in his arms all of twenty minutes before the phone rang. Grabbing it quickly before it awakened Orlando, I saw the name on the display. *What the hell?* It was a call from home—my sister, Joan. The last thing I wanted to hear after a wonderful night of unbridled sex and passion was judgemental Joan.

I answered in a sleepy voice. "Hello?"

"Candy?"

"What is it, Joan?"

A pause, then words that sounded so sincere. "Hey, sis, just wanted to call and wish you a happy anniversary."

"It was yesterday."

"I know I'm a little late, but, with a set of two-year-old twins, a seven-year-old, and a demanding husband, there is hardly any time for anything else."

"So, you and Jeff doing okay?"

"Great. What about you and Orlando."

"We're fine, thank you, despite what everyone up there may be thinking."

"That's why I called. I just wanted to let you know that I am proud of you. I knew all along that you could do it, Candy. You just needed the right man."

"Really? That's what you called for?"

"That's it. My days of condemning you are over and I wanted to let you know that. I miss my sister."

"You miss *me?*"

"Sure, stupid! How many sisters do you think I have?"

"There *is* Chris."

"Yeah, like she counts. No one ever hears from her unless its to announce her next child. She's too busy with those six kids to remember the rest of us. Which brings me to my next question. You're the only one of us without kids. I want other nieces and nephews, so when is it your turn? You two planning to add an Italian branch to the family tree?"

I answered slowly. "I have no idea, maybe in a year or two."

"I know you and that fine-ass husband get it on enough to have had kids by now."

If she only knew. But I wasn't going into details. "He's such a good husband. Joan. He's everything to me."

"Just don't forget that you still have me. I've gotta go before the twins wake up. Jeff needs his breakfast. Can you come and see me soon?"

I smiled a smile of contentment. "I'd love to, maybe after Orlando and I are set on our jobs. We just got our new apartment, and there's a lot I have to do around here. I should have gotten started yesterday, but I was a little . . . well, busy."

"So I imagine."

"If only you could. Orlando is really something!"

We said our good-byes. I made breakfast for a still-tired husband, treated him to another quickie then sent him on his way to make Florence more beautiful than it already was.

Take a sneak peek at PURE SEX, starring three hot new authors of contemporary erotica: Lucinda Betts, Bonnie Edwards, and Sasha White. Available in July 2006 from Aphrodisia . . .

Alone below, Teri took in how sumptuous the boat was. The website hadn't done it justice. Pleased, she noted an extra long cream-colored leather sofa along one side. A couple of armchairs completed the furnishings while a plasma screen television was set on the wall. Light wood cabinets kept the cooking area from being dark. She marveled at the ingenious use of space and opened every cupboard she saw.

The bathroom off the master cabin was small but well appointed with a shower set in a tiny tub. She opened the medicine chest over the sink to check out what it was that Jared had put away. A variety pack of condoms: glow in the dark, flavored and ribbed for her pleasure.

Extra large.

She snorted. Philip should be so lucky.

Back in the master cabin she checked out the drawer in the night table. The DVDs Jared had put away were X-rated. She popped one into the player, propped herself on the bed and skipped through the beginning to find couples enjoying strong, healthy, powerful sex. Great sex. Friendly sex. Even affectionate sex.

Philip's pious expression when he'd explained the concept of revirginizing swam in front of her mind's screen. He wanted them to remember their wedding night as special, he'd said.

She'd been amazingly agreeable. It had been so easy to give up sleeping with him; she should have seen the signs of a dying relationship.

But by then the wedding had taken on a life of its own, a juggernaut, there was no stopping it. His mother, her mother, the caterer, the church, the dress!

None of the energetic sex she saw on the portable bedroom television had ever happened with Philip. She sighed, wandered out to the little kitchen, retrieved the champagne from the fridge, opened it and poured herself a tumbler full. She considered digging out the flutes Jared had put away but the tumbler held more. And Teri wanted lots.

When she settled back onto the bed a couple onscreen were enjoying a fabulously decadent soixante-neuf. The actor's tongue work looked enthusiastic. The actress looked happy.

Teri watched closely, amused at first. The moaning and sex talk were obviously dubbed in afterward. No one really said things like that, no one felt things as strongly as the actors pretended.

She changed positions on the bed, lying on her belly with her head at the foot so she could see the action up close. And up close was what she got.

The camera closed in on his tongue so Teri could see the moisture, the red, full clit he was licking and sucking gently between his lips.

Her own body reacted to the visual stimulus and moistened as the actress widened her legs and the actor slid his tongue deep into her. She thrashed on the bed in a stunning display of sexual hysteria that had never, ever overcome her.

Teri was jealous. Did people react this strongly to oral sex? She never had. But, then, Philip was so fastidious she doubted he'd ever been as deeply involved as the actor was. Even an actor who was being paid to fake it was more turned on that Philip had been the few times she'd insisted.

Teri knew what she wanted, knew what she liked, knew what would get her off like a rocket, but Philip had issues.

She'd always hoped he'd warm up more. Get hotter, get horny. For her. But he hadn't. Wouldn't. Not ever.

The onscreen couple switched positions and the actress performed fellatio until the man bucked and howled with his orgasm. The couple tumbled onto the sofa, sated.

Teri clicked off the TV, took another long drink and rolled onto her back. Her legs slid open and she felt herself, moist and heavy with need.

The bedroom door was open and from here she could see through the living area and up the stairs to one small rectangular patch of sky. She wondered what would happen if Jared were to peer down the hatch and see her here with her legs splayed and her hand on her wet slit.

Would the pirate on the deck come down to the master cabin and grab her ankles like the actor had? She closed her eyes and let her fantasy play out. It was better than any porn flick because she could control every movement, every word and all of her responses. She could tell Jared what to do and he'd do it.

She could tell him to lick her breasts and lift her hips to bring her closer to his mouth. He could trail his scratchy chin delicately along her inner thigh until he got close enough that she could feel his hot breath on her hotter pussy. She slid her other hand to a nipple and plucked it while she opened to her questing fingertip.

She would tell him to linger there, just far enough away from her that he'd be able to see her wet lips, smell her aroused flesh, feel her need. Sliding a fingertip into herself, familiar tension built while she worked to bring herself to orgasm. He would kiss her there where she was hottest, moist and achy. He'd do whatever she told him to and like it.

She wasn't wired for abstinence, hadn't wanted to go along with Philip's crazy idea, but—oh, yes, it was building to a peak now and soon she'd be over the—on a weak sigh, her orgasm pulsed through her lower body in a poor imitation of what she'd witnessed onscreen.

She opened her eyes on the wish that Jared had seen her, that he was right now on his way to ravish her like the pirate he was. But no, he'd been a gentleman and left her to herself.

Her unsatisfied self.

She'd taken the edge off, but it had been far too long since she'd had a truly good orgasm. And she deserved one. Or three.

Or a week full of them. She smiled and rose to wash her hands. In the mirror, she faced herself.

Philip was gone. She was here. Jared was here.

And Jared was hot, hot, hot.

She decided to unpack her lingerie after all.

Her carryon bag sat on the floor beside the bed, tagged and zipped and bulging. A couple of sharp points threatened to poke holes through the sides, but still, she couldn't bring herself to open it.

She took another drink of champagne instead.

The bag was full of shoes. Stilettos, each and every pair. Toes pointed enough to cripple, Philip always wanted her to wear them. If he'd wanted a tall, lanky, long limbed wife why had he asked her out in the first place? She would never have that look, no matter how high her heels were. She was lean, yes, but her muscle tone was obvious.

Some men liked her athletic build. The pirate above deck for one, she realized as she poured and drank another tumbler of champagne. She sat on the edge of the bed, one toe on the floor for balance, the other heel tucked into her crotch. She bent over toward the night table to grab the bottle again, but nearly fell off the bed.

She was tipsy. Well and truly feeling no pain. She giggled.

Oh, hell, who cared? There was no one here to judge her. No one to tell her she'd had too much and had to mind herself.

No one to tell her to keep her hands to herself and off Jared MacKay.

"Step away from the pirate," she intoned in a dramatic imitation of Philip's most commanding tone. Then she laughed harder.

Philip had no say in anything she did anymore. He'd given up the right to chastise her, instruct her or humiliate her when he'd dashed out of the church this morning.

She stood, still laughing, curiously aware of an incredible sense of freedom. She set aside her carryon bag. She'd open it later. Right now she wanted her bathing suit and sarong.

There was a sunset waiting for her.

A sunset and a pirate who needed taming.

Hot cops and the women who love them, coming up in THE COP. Available October 2006 from Aphrodisia, featuring Sasha White, Alyssa Brooks, and Renée Alexis. Here's a scorching sneak peek at "Detroit's Finest," by Renée . . .

Minutes later, Troy slammed a file on top of the cabinet. "Damn!"

I looked at him with wide eyes. "Are you okay?"

"No, I'm not okay."

His hand slowly massaged his temple and I moved into him. "Troy, what is it?"

He faced me. "I can't lie to you, Tracey."

"What are you talking about?"

"You don't know how hard it is to be near you and not have you. Each time I look at you my body does what it wants to despite what my mind says."

I pressed on, loving what I was hearing, yet skittish about taking things out of context. But there was something about Troy that made me chuck my fear and take his hands into mine, console him, feel any part of him against me. I smiled at him and spoke softly. "You know, the first time I saw you I went hog wild, but I didn't know you. I just wanted to screw you and get satisfied in ways I knew only you could satisfy me. Then I actually met you. True, you were giving me a ticket but I had you in my grasp nonetheless. When you gave me my money back, I knew I wouldn't be able to hide my feelings . . . like now."

He moved so close into me that I could feel that powerful tenting erupting in his pants and wanted it throbbing deeply inside me. His words enticed me further. "Tell me what those feelings are."

"Explicitly?"

"That's the only way I want it from you."

I shrugged my shoulders. "I won't lie and say what you have in your pants isn't doing something for me because it is. The only thing I've ever wanted to do was hold you in my arms and claim you, but Daisha is in the way of that."

"She's not in the way down here."

"You wouldn't think badly of me kissing you?"

"I would if that's all you did to me."

"What do you want?"

"All of it. Everything!"

Troy laid his hat on the top of the file cabinet, then reached to loosen his tie. All along my eyes widened, hungered for every inch he could deliver to me. As I watched him slowly unbutton his dark shirt and loosen his belt, something exploded inside me, jacking my panties. I rode the wave and let those tiny electrons invade my body as he exposed his to me. My hands shook and I almost dropped to my knees when he slid his hand up and down a phallus that was ready to be uncovered and sucked into submission.

With his shirt dangling open and his hand rubbing his chest, he reached for me. "You take me the rest of the way because I can't wait to have your hands on me. The minute I saw you I knew this day was going to happen. I made it happen by following you down here. I almost made it happen the day I followed you to the mall but I chickened out."

"I imagined you making love to me as you gave me that sobriety test, but that's all it was, a daydream—until now."

"I know the feeling and I'm not running scared anymore, girl, I don't care who's upstairs waiting for me to return to her."

He pulled me into him and my body sizzled from contact with him. My fingers traced his lip line, barely able to fathom touching him. God, he was as soft as I imagined. I stared into his eyes while stroking his full lips and exposed chest. My hands were so busy that I hadn't time to think of my actions, didn't really care about anything other than what I was about to do with Mr. Troy . . . man of the hour, man of the day!

His lips nipped at my fingers, soon sucking them slowly, pretending his lips were mine covering a taut erection in slow, sucking movements. My other hand stroked pecs so strong and sinfully satin that my knees buckled. Was I really touching this man? The feel of his nipples as my nails tenderly raked against them proved that very potent point. My hand traced the muscles of his ribcage, then tapered to his stomach, circling his naval and toying with the band of his underwear. I could feel the heat from his engorged erection pressing against my palm, getting hotter and hotter, needing its flames dowsed. Gladly. I was already clinically insane from want. Why not take my gift and pamper it?

Our lips finally met and we drank from one another in fusion. Lips, tongues and desire got us higher as we intertwined, mating, pulling, sucking. His lips parted from mine and sucked my neck. His hands tightened around my behind, squeezing, rocking against me. His cock was so ready to plunge into me, please me, crack my code and I wanted him to so desperately.

Our lips met again as he raised my skirt, quickly finding the seat of my wet panties. He groaned as he slipped two fingers into my damp sex, rocking them into me the way his hips rocked against mine. He devoured me, slipping finger after finger around my clit, rubbing it, making it throb. Those same very active fingers stroked my labia, tracing the delicate folds with the tips of his fingers, making my juices flow. We parted and he stared at my flushed face, smiling. "This is so damn good, Tracey. I knew you had to feel like satin. My tip is so juiced for you that I can barely stand it."

His lips sucked mine again in long, lavish pulls and tugs, breathing against me as he screwed the daylights out of my sex with his fingers. I could barely hold back and he felt the same sensation within my body. "You ready to come, baby?

You ready to release that sweetness to me, tighten around me?"

"Troy! Please."

He worked his fingers into me harder, rougher until I collapsed and spilled my cream onto his waiting fingers. The more I came, the more he rocked me, kissed me, tightened his grip on my behind.

My fingers once again found his rod, stroked it through his pants material and I took him hard, cupping him. His tip moved within my grasp and I whispered, "Take it out, Troy and let me have it."

"You want it, baby?"

"Since day one."

He loosened his belt and zipper while I played in his hair, feeling the loose curls wrap around my fingers. I trailed the delicate hair on his neck and sideburns while staring into a face that was so magnificent. How could he be so incredible and not truly be mine? No answers to that impossible question, but I took what I had at the moment and played it well.

His exposed cock took me by storm. It was beautiful, straight and long, with veins in all the perfect places for deep satisfaction. My mouth watered from the sight of it. It glistened from moisture, his tip sprinkled from need of release and I dropped to my knees to give it what it had to have. I stared up at him. "She must give it to you all the time, as pretty as it is."

"I hardly get it."

"You want it now?"

"Right now, baby. Give me everything your pretty ass can possibly give me."

I had to take him, all of him right way. I went so deep on him that he immediately tickled the back of my throat. I looked up at him in time enough to see his head rear back, eyes tighten from pleasure, jaws clenching as insane words erupted from him, "Take it, girl, suck it! Suck it hard, baby-girl."

That was my clue. I waxed him good by sliding my wicked tongue around his tip and underside of it. His thick veins tickled my tongue, making me salivate from his taste. He was wickedly delicious.

His hands played in my long strands, forcing my mouth deeper onto him as he readied himself for the ultimate release. His fingers strummed my cheeks. "I'm so ready, baby, so ready to give you what I have. Do you want it?"

"Every inch—deep and hard, Troy."

He pulled that fabulous member from me and I watched it dangle and waiver in the air, so tight with liquid love that he could barely walk. He pulled me to my feet and pointed to the rug a few feet away. "I wish this was a more comfortable place for us because you deserve better, but I can't wait."

I kissed his lips again. "I can't wait either." At that, I lay on the rug and awaited his entrance. Troy mounted me, and my legs automatically surrounded him. My arms wrapped around his bare back as he unbuttoned my blouse and lowered my bra. His lips met with the first tender nipple and tugged on it, making it perkier with each caress. Inside, my body howled as he licked down my chest and stomach, and tugged my skirt and panties. Immediately, his tongue circled the curls of my pubic hair. I wanted his tongue inside me, circling me, eating me ruggedly, forcefully—any way Troy wanted to take me.

He fingered me, making me wetter than I thought imaginable, making me long for his penetration. Once again, he kissed my lips then stood to his knees, bringing my sex near to his tip. He massaged the garters holding my sheer stockings and smiled. "I've always wanted a woman who wore sexy things like this."

His entrance was so smooth and quick, forcing everything inside me in one thrust. He trembled with contact of my dew, sliding so tightly inside me that he had to bite his own lip not to scream!

As he rocked my soaking sex, his lips on mine matched his motion, kissing and talking as he rocked me to my very core. "This is so damn good, Tracey and I've wanted you for so long. Five fucking months of aching for you but it was so well worth the wait."